A Dreadful Penance

Jason Vail

A DREADFUL PENANCE

A Hawk Publishing book.

ISBN-13: 978-1470083342
ISBN-10: 1470083345

Hawk Publishing
Tallahassee, FL 32312

A Dreadful Penance

NOVEMBER 1262

Chapter 1

"I tell you, war's coming," growled Sir Geoffrey Randall, the coroner of Herefordshire, losing his patience. "I can feel it."

"That's your gout acting up, Geoff," shouted one of the knights further down the dinner table.

"My gout's fine, I'll have you know," Sir Geoff snapped. "Llywelyn ap Gruffydd is gathering an army. I heard it again this morning."

"Did that red-haired girl at the Wobbly Kettle whisper it in your ear?" the knight shouted back.

Sir Geoff scowled. Such sharp talk could often lead to trouble, but he and the knight had known each other since they were children, and had wrestled and fought together many times. So the scowl was not because he was angry, but because he could not overcome doubt.

"No," he said, "I got it in the Beast's Market at Galdeford Gate."

"What? The Welsh have sent out criers to spread the news?"

"From a drover," Sir Geoff said.

"What do drovers know?" replied Guy de Corsham, the sheriff.

"He came in from Powys with a herd of cattle for sale," Sir Geoff said. "He said that Llywelyn had called the muster."

"Just talk," someone said.

"So what?" one of the others said. "Barefoot rabble, the lot of them."

"You weren't here six years ago when Llywelyn came out of the hills the last time," Sir Geoff said. "Barefoot many may be and a rabble, but a dangerous rabble."

"It's the wrong season for fighting," yet another said. "No one goes to war in November. The rains turn the roads to mud if it doesn't snow first. You can't move an army over muddy roads."

"It has been quiet on the border, I'll give you that," Corsham said. "Damned quiet. Too quiet."

"Exactly," Sir Geoff said. "Our Prince of Wales can only be planning trouble." Ordinarily, the end of the threshing in late October and early November brought a season of raid and counter raid. Yet no word of any such raids had reached the ears about the table.

There were snorts at the reference to Llywelyn as Prince of Wales. Wales in the best of times was an ungovernable land, split into many little powers that warred with each other as much as with the English. That disunity was one of the main reasons that England had been able to subdue much of south Wales. But the north remained untamed, and now this Llywelyn had arisen and brought enough unity to the north that he had the temerity to call himself prince of all the Welsh. And he was not weak. He had taken back the Four Cantreds in north Wales, land held by the English, and he had greater ambitions than the independence of Gwynedd and Powys.

"Perhaps," Sir Geoff said, "they have all gone to the muster."

"We'll know there's trouble afoot when Mortimer calls a muster," said another of the knights at the table. The reference was to Roger Mortimer, the most powerful of the border lords. His seat lay at the great Wigmore castle only nine miles away from where they sat in the great hall of Ludlow castle.

"You'll know there's trouble afoot when the Welsh are burning down your hayricks and firing your barns," Sir Geoff said.

But the talk moved on, as dinner table talk always does, meandering from subject to subject at whim and chance.

Down at the end of the table, Stephen Attebrook, the deputy coroner, glanced toward the clerk at his side, Gilbert Wistwode. Stephen rated space at the table because he was a knight and Sir Geoff's subordinate; Gilbert because he was Sir Geoff's clerk. The occasion for the dinner was the sheriff's and Sir Geoff's attendance at the area's hundred court. Their presence was mostly for ceremony. The sheriff made the rounds of all the hundred courts in the county twice a year to formally accept presentments in cases that required a referral to the king's justices, and informally to keep his finger on the pulse of things. And this sheriff was new. He had been appointed only last spring, so he had a lot of pulses to check. This part of England was pretty solid for King Henry, but there were still those who supported the rebellious barons who looked for leadership to Simon de Montfort, the man who had forced the king to accept the Provisions of Oxford which limited his powers. These men had to be detected and watched, for although the king had thrown off the provisions, he was weak and the reformers were gathering strength for another go.

"You know," Gilbert said softly so that only Stephen could hear, "I wondered why it was so easy to get there and back unmolested." Just a month ago, Gilbert had undertaken a dangerous journey deep into Wales on Stephen's behalf to deliver his son to a Welsh cousin for safekeeping.

Stephen frowned, alarmed that his boy, Christopher, was not so safe after all. When armies marched, no one nearby was safe, even if the army was your own. He had a great deal of experience in this, having just returned from nine years of fighting in Spain.

"They're far from the border," Gilbert hastened to add, reading Stephen's expression. "Trouble won't find them there."

"I need to get him back," Stephen said.

"I suppose so," Gilbert said. "You'll be going alone?"

Stephen smiled. "Ah, yes. You'll be busy. The latrine needs to be burned out again."

"It could use a dose of flame," Gilbert said, eyes shifting back and forth as he recalled a secret sunk in that latrine: the body of a man who had come to kill Stephen and been killed himself instead. Gilbert was a bald, stout man unused to fighting and riding. The prospect of a ride of any distance filled Gilbert with dismay, and the notion of a ride into darkest Wales, which had bandits behind every bush, was less attractive now than it had been a month ago.

Stephen sighed. "I guess I'll have to take Harry."

"He does not ride well either," Gilbert said.

"He rides better than you," Stephen said. In fact, Harry, a legless beggar who lived in the stables of the Broken Shield Inn, did not ride at all as far as either of them knew. He clumped around on a flat piece of wood with rockers on the bottom and thick leather gloves to protect his hands.

"That is unkind."

"To compare him with you, I know."

"I shall remember this, I really shall."

"And do what? Put lice in my bed? There are already more there than can inhabit it comfortably."

"Our beds are not lousy," Gilbert said a bit too loud, for eyes turned in his direction. Gilbert, or rather his wife Edith, was the proprietor of one of the best inns in Ludlow, the Broken Shield, where Stephen currently lived in a drafty, cramped room at the top floor normally reserved for servants or storage. Stephen didn't mind too much, since he had the room to himself, a luxury not often available to the inhabitants of inns, and it was free.

Servants appeared with bowls of water and towels for the men at table to wash their hands, signifying that dinner was over.

When the tables had been cleared away and stacked in another room, court resumed in the hall. Stephen had no more to do with the proceedings in the afternoon than he had in the morning. His role was to stand behind Sir Geoff's chair; not that Sir Geoff had that much to do himself. His work had been done in the morning, and now he and the sheriff merely observed while the hundred bailiff and the hundred jury took care of matters.

It wasn't long before Stephen's feet began to ache again, especially his bad one, which a Moorish axe had shortened atop a castle wall in Spain. It seemed the afternoon would never end, filled with a continuing procession of little cases — disputes about fights; the theft of some chickens; despoliation by pigs allowed onto someone's property causing a devastating loss of turnips; a freeman plowing up a villein's field strips for his own use; the carrying off of someone's firewood; a man beating his wife too severely in the opinion of the neighbors and the bailiff; a woman beating her husband over the head with a bucket. The stuff of everyday life in the country, familiar and comfortable. Stephen might have listened more attentively but the pain was too distracting.

At last the end came, and the bailiff rose and adjourned the court. The crowd lingered, for this court, like any court, was an opportunity to socialize.

Stephen should have stayed. It had been a long time since he had been home and he had a lot of catching up to do with people in the region. But his thoughts were on a distant child and getting the weight off his feet, a massage for his bad foot to take out the kinks, and a pot of ale by the fire in the Broken Shield.

He spotted Gilbert in conversation with a wealthy peasant who had complained about someone damming his stream. Stephen had hoped for company on the walk back, but clearly it was not to be. He said good bye to Sir Geoff, who had acquired a pewter cup of wine. Sir Geoff nodded in response as he sniffed the wine with an appraising air, barely looking up.

The cramped inner bailey of Ludlow castle smelled of rain, wet stone and damp wool, and when Stephen passed into the vast outer bailey, the aroma changed to horse manure from the big paddock to the right. Stephen was so used to the smell he hardly noticed it. And his attention was on the sky, for the gray cloud cover of the last few weeks, which had brought constant if light rain, had broken open to reveal a sky that remarkably was still blue. The last afternoon sun took advantage of the change of weather to throw down a golden cloak of light.

Stephen sniffed the air. "I believe it's getting warmer," he said to himself as he went through the gate into the town. People said that the winters were colder than when he was a small child, and they had not been looking forward to this one, since the harvest had been short and food was expected to be scarce. Perhaps this warm snap would grow and last, and the winter would not be a hardship after all.

Abreast of Mill Street, he passed the Wattepas house, where the journeymen and apprentice goldsmiths were hard at work, visible through the open windows. The formidable Mistress Wattepas was in the door and returned his greeting with a polite nod, not that she held any warmth for him after that business a few months ago with her former maid.

Stephen paused at the top of Broad Street. The town looked so fresh and fine, bathed in the afternoon's golden light. Up and down both High Street and Broad, all the shutters were open as if it were summer and he could see people moving within, going about their business.

He had been a child at a fortified manor to the northwest, and he could remember when the Welsh came raiding: the mournful clanging of the alarm bell at the arrival of the messenger; the sudden panic at the sound of it; the rushing about; the manor's folk streaming in from the village with only the goods they could carry, possessions dropped along the way leaving a trail of litter to mark the refugees' passage; his mother and Tim the blacksmith fumbling to dress his father in mail, dropping the coif in their haste and fumbling with the ties; his father's fierce expression as he waited impatiently; then father stalking out of the house, resplendent in mail from head to foot, blue-and-white shield on his back and helmet under his arm; the women and men and boys without arms in the hall, a pall of anxiety as thick as porridge in the air; how he had slipped out a window and run to the top of the embankment to peer through the gaps in the palisade, hoping for a glimpse of the enemy. Father had caught him there, but for a change had said nothing at his disobedience. The Welsh had not come to Hafton during his childhood, but they had seen smoke columns in the distance that marked the lands the raiders had visited.

If the Welsh were gathering an army, more would be lost than some cattle, a few hayricks and part of the harvest. Stephen thought about the savage Welsh swarming over the walls and sacking Ludlow: of fires burning everywhere, people running and screaming, men dragged into the street to be butchered, women and girls to be raped, all the goods of all the houses strewn about like so much wreckage. He had seen such things more than once and had done his share of pillaging — it was the best way for a poor soldier to gain wealth, after all. He did not wish such a fate on peaceful Ludlow and the people he knew, or on anyone else. He hoped Sir Geoff was wrong.

At last he reached Bell Lane and turned in. The Broken Shield sat only a few long strides down a lane so narrow that he practically had to flatten himself against a building wall to get out of the way of an ox cart headed toward Broad Street.

He entered the inn, mindful to wipe his feet on the mat so as not to invoke the wrath of Edith Wistwode or her daughter Jennie, who were demons to anyone who dared to dirty the inn's floor. It was made of wood and very costly, one of the few such floors in town.

It was early enough that no one had taken his favorite spot between the fire and the stairs. He settled onto a bench as Nan, one of the maid servants, deposited a clay cup of ale on the table.

The best way to get into Wales without being noticed was to stay off the roads, he thought as he sipped the ale and stared out the window. He had never snuck into Wales before, but he had slipped into Grenada a time or two. It couldn't be much different. He began to think about how he would do it and what he would take with him.

Stephen had his boot off and was massaging the stump of his bad foot when the Shield's door banged open and Gilbert hurried over, leaving dirty footprints on the floor.

Stephen had time to note the grim expression on his face. Gilbert said in the grave tone that he employed only when announcing a death: "Sir Geoff needs you right away."

"Ah, Stephen, there you are," Sir Geoff said as Stephen and Gilbert slipped into the room. "I wondered where you had got to."

They were in the lower chamber of one of the west towers overlooking the River Teme. Stephen looked about for a dead man, but all the bodies in the room were on their feet and quite alive.

"Stephen," Sir Geoff went on, "may I present Prior Hugh."

Prior Hugh sat on a cushioned chair opposite Sir Geoff, both of them by the fire where they could enjoy the best of the heat from the single fireplace cut into the walls. It was hard to gauge his height, but he seemed a small man. He had the sharp face of a clerk, handsome despite the clefts on either side of his mouth. The austerity of the face, however, was offset by dark eyes that seemed as though they could glow with warmth but now were filled with anxiety and concern, and unruly hair tinged with gray that, although it appeared an attempt had been made to tame it with a comb, fell in thick ringlets from the bare tonsure at the dome of his skull.

He wore the habit of an Augustinian monk, and he was not the only one so dressed in the room. Two other monks stood by the slit window overlooking the Teme. But they evidently were not important enough to rate an introduction.

"Your honor," Stephen said, "a pleasure."

Hugh nodded, but did not look Stephen in the eye and did not seem the least glad to meet him.

"Stephen is my deputy," Sir Geoff said.

"How fortunate," said Hugh.

"He will provide you will all the assistance you require."

"I had hoped for . . ." Hugh let his words die.

"For what?"

"Well, that you might come yourself."

"I am in no condition to undertake such a journey. And besides, what would be the point? It's outside my jurisdiction. I cannot leave the county."

"It isn't far."

"It is farther than I am prepared to go."

"Of course," Hugh said politely, accepting the rebuff.

"He has a habit for getting into trouble, but has proven himself adept at finding things out, it seems." Sir Geoff squinted at Stephen. "Or so I've been told."

"I suppose."

"It's the best I can do."

"But our priory!" Hugh said, giving way to agitation. "This matter could destroy us!"

"What matter?" Stephen asked.

Sir Geoff fixed him with a glare. "One of Prior Hugh's monks has been murdered and he wants to find out who is responsible."

"He died in bed," Gilbert said as he warmed himself by the fire after the monks had withdrawn.

Sir Geoff glowered as if a secret had been improvidently revealed, although the matter was certainly not a secret between them.

"That's what one of the brothers told me," Gilbert hastened to add. "I don't know about you, but I hope to die in bed myself, although rather more gently." He shuddered. "A cut throat, a most unpleasant way to go."

"Better that than hanging," Sir Geoff said, with the aristocrat's aversion to the rope.

"I can't go," Stephen said from the other side of the room, far from the fire, where the cold of autumn seeped from the stone walls.

"What do you mean you can't go?" Sir Geoff said.

"I have other business."

"What other business?"

"A family matter."

"I am family, damn it," Sir Geoff said. He was, in fact, a distance cousin by marriage to his third wife. Everyone who lived in this part of the county seemed to be related somehow or other. "And I'm ordering you to go."

Stephen smiled without humor at the idea of being ordered about by a relative, even one so distant. Relatives asked for favors; they did not dispatch orders as if to a servant. "As you said, the priory is in Shropshire and outside your jurisdiction. You can't order me to do anything there."

Sir Geoff slapped the arm of his chair. "Don't get legal on me."

"He is a lawyer," Gilbert said, "well, almost one. I suppose he can't help it."

"No wonder Valence finds you such a trial," Sir Geoff fumed. Ademar de Valence was a crown circuit justice whose territory embraced this part of England. Years ago, Stephen had been Valence's clerk, and more recently had a bitter dispute with him over the finding of a missing list of the names of supporters of de Montfort. Stephen had sent his son into Wales because of Valence.

"He's been complaining about me," Stephen said.

"At length," Gilbert said.

"How would you know?" Stephen said. "Eavesdropping?"

"No," Gilbert said, "he shouted so loudly that I could hear him through the door."

"And you never had your ear pressed against it, I'm sure."

"Enough!" Sir Geoff shouted. He took several deep breaths. "Stephen, this is important to me. My first wife endowed the priory. Her body is buried there. I hope to be buried there — beside her."

And if the priory collapses, no one will be there to tend your graves or say prayers for you, Stephen thought. But the prospect of pillagers forcing their way into his Welsh cousin's house where his boy now lived left him unmoved by the danger to Sir Geoff's soul.

Before Sir Geoff could say more, Gilbert spoke up with almost as much heat. "Hugh is right — this matter could tear the priory apart. Suspicion is a terrible thing. It's corrosive. The priory is held together only because of the trust the men have in each other and their love of God. No one knows why this man died. The others may fear the same thing for themselves. Before long, they will start to leave, if they haven't already."

Gilbert's emotion surprised Stephen until he remembered that Gilbert had been a monk himself once, long ago, before he met Edith, yielded to temptation and married her.

"I gave you an opportunity when you had nothing," Sir Geoff said ominously, gripping the arms of the chair as if he might tear them loose.

Stephen had indeed returned to England last summer with very little: his arms and armor, three horses, a small son, a maimed foot and a cargo of grief so large that it seemed that nothing could heal the wound. With the maimed foot, he thought he had no hope of being taken on even as a hired knight. So Sir Geoff's offer of help, small as it was, had come as a relief. He was grateful, but the implied threat of discharge had the opposite effect, for it hardened him against compliance, as threats usually did.

As if sensing Stephen's mood, Gilbert said, "You go to the priory, Stephen. I will fetch the boy for you."

"I can't let you do that," Stephen said. "It's too dangerous."

"I made it before," Gilbert said.

"I shouldn't have sent you even then. It was madness, thoughtless. If you go again and suffer harm, Edith will never forgive me."

"I had no idea you valued her good opinion," Gilbert said.

"She is frightful and you are not," Stephen said.

"What are you talking about?" Sir Geoff asked, confused.

Gilbert answered, "Last month, when Valence sought the missing list of the king's supporters and his enemies in this part of the country, he seized Stephen's son for his good behavior, hoping to ensure Stephen's best efforts to recover the list. Stephen stole the boy back and dispatched me with him to a relative deep in Powys for safekeeping. Didn't Valence tell you about this?"

"No, he didn't," Sir Geoff said.

"It's so unlike our justice to color the truth," Stephen said.

"Nor did either of you," Sir Geoff growled. "This is the first time I've heard of it."

Gilbert went on: "So Stephen fears for the boy's safety now that war is brewing."

"You rode into Wales alone?" Sir Geoff asked, astonished.

Gilbert nodded.

"And you propose to do it again? Now?"

"It seems the only way," Gilbert said.

Sir Geoff's eyes narrowed and flicked from one man to the other. His lips parted and he drew a breath to speak.

Before he could give an opinion on this plan, Stephen said, "I will go to the priory. I will do your business there. Then I will fetch Christopher." His words came grimly, as if to say them was a great effort. He smiled at Gilbert. "Edith will have my skin off if you go. No doubt by this time, she's heard the rumors."

"Excellent." Sir Geoff slapped the arms of his chair. Now that resistance had vanished, his anger evaporated as well. "You leave tomorrow."

He paused, then added, "There is one other task I need you to perform."

"What, sir?" Stephen asked cautiously.

"It may interfere with your plans."

"How so?"

"There is a horse trader named Llwyn at Clun. He often has reason to go into Wales, and when he does, he is remarkably good at gathering intelligence. I want you to engage him to undertake such a journey and learn, if he can, what Llywelyn is up to."

"He would do that?"

"For money, he will."

"I could do it just as well, and more cheaply."

"I doubt the Welsh will suffer an Englishman to ride around the countryside chatting people up. They'll have your head off at the first place you stop. This fellow, though, he's as Welsh as they come. No one is likely to bother him. You clean up this business at the priory as best you can while you wait for him to get back. Dispatch Gilbert here with a letter containing the man's news about Llywelyn's intentions. Then you can run around Wales to your heart's content."

Chapter 2

In the dream, he was on top of the castle wall again in Spain. Arrows were falling everywhere, making tink-tink noises when they struck stone — a pattering of deadly rain — and thunks when they struck the defenders' shields.

He heard the thumps of the scaling ladders as their tops collided with the wall and the shout from the Moors below which encouraged the assault parties.

Stephen took up a long pole with a Y-shaped end which was used to push away the ladders. In the dream, the pole either slipped off the top rung, or when he managed to get the ladder away from the wall, it simply slapped back no matter how much he wrestled with it, and the Moors kept coming.

His woman Taresa was there behind him shouting that he was an idiot and that he should push harder. But in the real attack, she had been in the hall with the families of the defenders and Christopher, who was too small to walk.

The first Moor gained the top of the wall. In the dream, he was a big man with an axe instead of a sword. In life, Stephen had mounted between the crenellations to engage him because he had leaned his shield against the wall to wield the pole and safety only lay in coming to grips with the enemy. When he had done so, the man following him, armed with an axe, had cut off part of his foot. In the dream, though, the Moor cut as his head and Stephen's arms were too heavy and slow to bring his sword into the high shield; they just hung at his sides while he watched the morning sun glint off the curved blade of the axe.

But the blow did not land. He awoke first, as he always did.

"Good lord!" a voice said in the darkness of his room. "Be careful there!"

It took a moment to register that the voice belonged to Gilbert, his face illuminated by a single candle.

Stephen looked down and realized he had his dagger in his hand. He returned the dagger to its sheath. He swung his feet out of bed. "Sorry." He squinted at the window. No sign of dawn showed there. "What time is it?"

"Just before dawn," Gilbert said. "I came to wake you. The prior wants to get an early start."

"Does he," Stephen said, considering how to tell the prior what he could do with his early start. It was cold in the room, and Stephen would have liked nothing better than to lay under the blankets for a few hours more. There were often nights when he did not sleep well, when his memories crept out of the locked place where he stored them against examination to disturb his sleep, nights like the one just passing. He got little rest on such nights, and the following day was often torture. Last night, the prospect of the long ride to Clun had seemed almost a holiday, but at the moment, the prospect filled him with dismay.

"I say," Gilbert asked, "are you all right? You were moaning."

"Nonsense. That must have been the wind."

"I didn't hear any wind. I am certain it was you."

"You are mistaken. Are you going to stand there and watch me prance around naked? Or did you come to help me dress?"

"I think you can handle that chore well enough yourself."

Gilbert paused at the door. "You shout, you know, sometimes. During the night."

"I do not."

"It disturbs the guests." He shut the door.

After Gilbert had gone, Stephen arose and cracked the shutters. There was a wind blowing and he immediately closed them, the goose pimples erupting all over. He poured water from the pitcher on the small table into the bowl, wet a rag and began to wash. The water was almost as cold as the air. The paying guests got warm water in the morning for an extra charge, but as Stephen lived rent free he had to make do with cold water, which did not help the goose pimples. He could have had warm, he supposed, but that would have cost him, and he had little money to spare.

When he had finished toweling off, he dressed and dared to crack the shutters again. Dawn was breaking now and although it was light enough to see the yard below and the roofs of the neighboring houses, there was about half an hour left still to sunrise. So it was no surprise that the stable doors below were still shut, signifying that Harry, who lived in a corner of the stable, had not yet risen.

The hall downstairs was deserted except for a boy on his knees attempting to convince the fire to reawaken by tossing dry twigs on the embers.

Stephen went through the narrow passageway beside the great stone block of the fireplace to the kitchen. Edith Wistwode was there with the cook. It was unusual for Edit to be up at this hour, although she was one of the earliest risers. Oat porridge was bubbling in a pot over a fire that had been going for some time, judging from the lively state of its embers.

"Is it soft yet?" Stephen asked about the porridge.

"Soft enough for the likes of you, I suppose," Edith said. She spooned him a bowl

"Can I have two?"

"At once?"

"I thought I would feed the Harry," he said, as if Harry were a dog, "since I've got to go to the stables."

"That will save Jennie some time."

She filled another wood bowl with porridge and put a spoon in it.

Stephen accepted the second bowl and spotted bacon crisped in a pan sitting by the fire. He sprinkled some on the porridge, under Edith's disapproving glare.

"That is for Gilbert," she said.

"He won't miss it. He's too fat as it is."

"Gilbert is not fat."

"Of course he is. You feed him too well," Stephen said, pausing to add some salt to the porridge before he went out. Porridge without salt was foul, but porridge properly cooked with salt and bacon was as near to heaven as you could get in the morning, wanting only cheese to make the delight complete.

He pulled open the stable door and went in. It was too dark to see anything inside, but Stephen knew the lay of it so well that he had no doubt of being able to find his way without bumping into anything or falling over. The stables consisted of a series of wicker-walled stalls stretching left and right, where guests could stable their animals at an extra charge. Harry inhabited a stall at the end on the left that was also used for storing hay.

"Harry," he asked, "you awake yet?"

"No. Go away. It's not time to get up."

"I bring food."

"Food, did you say? What kind of food?"

"The usual. Edith's famous oat porridge."

"If Edith's porridge is famous, it's only for breaking people's teeth." If porridge was not fully cooked, the cracked oat grains remained hard. At times, they could feel like pebbles.

"You still have teeth left?"

"You know I have a full mouth of teeth."

"It's hard to know what you've got hidden behind that beard of yours," Stephen said as he reached the stall and met Harry. Although it was difficult to see at the moment, Harry's beard was a huge, shaggy thing that hung to his chest. With his unruly mass of brown hair, uncombed and uncut in years, the only things normally visible about his face were his eyes and nose.

"There is nothing wrong with my beard. It helps keep me warm in these cold days."

Harry accepted the bowl in a way that did not fail to convey a sense of disappointment. Most days, Jennie Wistwode delivered his breakfast. Mealtimes were the only moments she paid any attention to him, and occasionally she even paused to exchange word or two.

Harry ate a spoonful, as did Stephen when he stood up. Harry said with some astonishment, "There's salt and bacon here."

"Well, don't choke on it."

"Huh," Harry grunted, mouth too full to talk as he rapidly devoured the bowl. Harry ate faster than any man Stephen had ever met, as if he expected the bowl to be snatched from his fingers before he had a chance to finish.

Harry finished the porridge, put the bowl on the ground and looked up at Stephen.

"No, you can't have mine," Stephen said. "I have a long way to go today and I need my strength."

"Where are you going?"

"Clun."

Harry paused. "I've heard a thing or two about Clun lately."

"What would that be?"

"Seems a monk turned up dead in his bed. Foul play, it's said."

"So you know about that?"

"A bit."

"I wouldn't think you'd care much for Shropshire gossip."

"Dead monks are often a matter of interest, especially murdered ones. You wouldn't happen to be going to Clun because of that?"

"No, I'm going for a view of the castle. I'm told it's very pretty."

"It's just a castle like any other," Harry snorted. "Nothing special."

"You've seen it then?"

"A few times."

"Really?" Stephen said, a bit surprised. Harry had been a farmer before the accident that had claimed his legs and farmers did not tend to stray much farther than the nearest market town. "What were you doing up there?"

"I fancied a girl."

"It's hard to imagine a girl fancying you."

"She fancied me fine. It was her father and brothers that were the problem. Now, if you've come to insult me, go about your business. I am a busy man and I must get dressed to face the day."

"Insult you? I was just making conversation."

"Then converse. Why are you really going to Clun? You're not looking for work, are you? Sir Geoff let you go? Serves you right. Can't trust a reckless fellow like you with crown business."

"Sir Geoff is friends with the prior and the prior asked for his help."

"So he's sending you? Not much of a helpful gesture, if you ask me. You'll just burn something down." This was a reference to Stephen's involvement in the burning of a certain Will Thumper's barn last month.

"If you know anything about Clun, perhaps you've heard of a fellow named Llwyn," Stephen said.

"Llwyn," Harry said. "Sounds foreign. Is he Welsh?"

"No, he's Estonian," Stephen said. "Of course, he's Welsh. A drover and horse trader at Clun."

"It seems to me that I've heard that name. Are you thinking about selling one of those nags of yours while you're up there? A poor man like you could support himself for a long time on the price of one of them."

"Maybe."

It was much lighter now and Stephen could see Harry's eyes narrow in calculation.

Harry said, "You know, my head's spinning so with hunger that it's hard to recall things."

"Why, Harry, you've just eaten. You should be refreshed and ready for the day."

"If I had another bowl of porridge I might remember better."

Stephen collected Harry's bowl. "I suppose I can manage that."

"And make sure that it has salt and bacon. And have Jennie bring it out."

Stephen saddled his mare and Gilbert's mule, and loaded his gear on the younger mare while he waited for Harry to finish. Harry was in no hurry because Jennie tarried so she could collect the bowl and avoid having to make another trip to the stables.

On her way out, Jennie flashed Stephen a quick smile. She was a bit on the thick side like her parents and no raving beauty, but she was good to look at just the same, and with her sunny personality she did not lack for attention. She was sixteen now and not yet married, and prospective suitors swarmed around on Sundays, annoying her parents a great deal.

As Stephen tied the horses and mule to one of the iron rings nailed into the outside wall of the stables, Harry clumped out the door.

He did not pause or glance at Stephen, but swung toward the gate.

"Not so fast," Stephen said.

"What is it?" Harry snapped. "The sun's almost up. If I wait any longer that dimwit Gip will have the gate open and I'll miss the morning traffic." Like all beggars in town, he had a license and his spot was at Broad Gate, where Gip was the warden. This was a market day, and by dawn the nearby farmers and traders would be lined up to get into town before the gates opened.

"I paid for your time," Stephen protested.

"You paid for my conversation, which is a priceless commodity by the way. We can have that anywhere," Harry said without stopping.

Harry could move with surprising speed for a man whose legs were off at the knees, and he was already at the gate before Stephen caught up with him. They turned into Bell Lane and headed toward Broad Street.

"So," Stephen began, hands behind his back and head up, not looking at Harry, as if the two of them just happened to be strolling along Bell Lane at the same time. Mistress Bartelot regarded them from her upper story window, as she regarded all the coming and going in Bell Lane every morning of every day. Her eyes met Stephen's, and he waved. She returned the wave, but not the smile that went with it, her face as grave as ever.

"Good morning!" Harry called to her.

Mistress Bartelot looked startled that Harry had spoken to her and disappeared from the window.

"So," Stephen continued, "what about that Llwyn fellow?"

"What about him?"

"What do you know?"

"He and his sons come through here every autumn with a herd of cattle and horses for the big market at Hereford. In fact, they were here in September just after you turned up. You didn't notice?"

"I'm afraid not."

Harry snorted. "And you call yourself a finder. A fly could land on the end of your nose and you'd miss it."

"I don't call myself anything. That's Gilbert's label."

"And I bet he tells you you're wonderful in other ways too, the flatterer." Harry paused, as they had reached the corner with Broad Street. He shook his great arms, gathered a breath and swung out into the street. "All right, as to this Llywn. I've seen him, mind, but all I know about him is what the gossips say, and you know how much weight you can put on that."

"No faults unexamined and every one magnified," Stephen murmured.

"I only tell what I've heard," Harry said. "I never embellish anything."

"Of course not."

"And only when I'm forced to by inquisitive folk."

"Naturally. Please go on."

"Certainly. He's a sharp dealer, but so is practically every other merchant. He breeds and sells horses, and is a factor for cattle brought in from Wales — takes them from the owners and drives them to market for a fee. But that's only his honest business, or so it is said."

"His honest business," Stephen repeated.

"That's what I said. The land north and east of Clun is safe enough — the knights' fees for the castle garrison lie one against the other there so that the Clun road is fairly safe. But west? You're in the land of highwaymen. It's not safe there. It's said that Llywn traffics with them, buys their goods and gives them shelter. He's not a man to be trusted in anything, if you get my meaning. A hard, dangerous man. Why do you really want to know, anyway? This isn't about your nags."

"No, it isn't."

"What's going on?"

"None of your business."

Harry looked insulted that anything should be considered none of his business, especially business of Stephen's. "That's the last time I share a confidence with you."

"No, it won't. You can't help yourself. You're too easily bought."

Harry squinted as he rolled along. "Well, a man's got to make a living."

"I know, Harry. Good day to you."

Stephen turned back and headed up Broad Street to the Broken Shield to fetch Gilbert and his horses for the trip to Clun.

"You're welcome!" shouted Harry, who always had to have the last word.

Chapter 3

Stephen and Gilbert had been told to meet the prior at the Beasts Market, the name given to the intersection of High and Old Streets near Galdefort Gate, so called because a market for trading in animals was held once a month within the great expanse where the two streets came together.

Stephen searched for the prior, but the triangular intersection was a swarm of activity, full of shouting and the clamor of animals amid temporary enclosures that had been thrown up all about. The place was so jammed with people and cattle, sheep, pigs and horses, that he could not find the prior.

A herd of cattle coming down Old Street from the gate forced everyone against the walls of the houses so that some people were nearly crushed. One twig of a woman selling hats balanced in a column on her head only survived by pressing the pointed handle of a wooden spoon against the flanks of any cow that got close enough to step on her as she stood back against a wall. Why a woman hat-seller would go about armed with a wooden spoon was a mystery, but Stephen was grateful that she had not been killed and that he had not had to delay his departure to summon a jury to probe that wonder. An even great mystery was how she had avoided spilling the hats in all the commotion.

After the herd passed, the herdsmen cracking whips and pushing the cows with staves into the largest of the temporary enclosures, Stephen finally caught a glimpse of the prior and his two monks in conversation with a knight on the other side of Old Street.

"It is a dangerous road, but we shall be safe enough," the knight declared as Stephen drew close enough to hear the conversation. "We shall be a large party. No robber will dare to bother us."

"Yes," said Prior Hugh. "But you're sure you cannot spare us a man for the leg to Clun?"

"I am not going that way, and I will not spare a man," the knight said. "The road to Shrewsbury is far more hazardous than the lands around Clun."

"Yes, yes," the prior conceded, worry in his voice.

Stephen understood the knight's concern. He had been up the road to Shrewsbury before, and he had had no trouble even when alone, but of late a band of robbers had been plaguing traffic along its length. It was said that there was no safety except with others.

The knot of travelers stood out from the swirling commotion like a clot of weed caught in an eddy of a fast current. There were easily two dozen people assembled at the northwest side of the intersection of Old and High Streets: the knight and his wife and children and armed escort and numerous pack horses; an elderly woman with a groom and two maids; a pair of brawny archers, their unstrung bows hanging from their shoulders in linen sacks; a carpenter and mason with their tools piled in a small handcart; and a company of players, all of whom had swords and many of whom looked as though they had had too much to drink last night, and whose own cart took up much space in the market, to the resenting glances of some of the merchants. Not all were going to the same place, but they were all going in the same direction, so they banded together for safety. An agent had gone around the inns of Ludlow last evening announcing that a packet would be leaving for Shrewsbury at dawn and this motley was what he had drawn.

"If you are so concerned about highwaymen, how did you dare come to Ludlow?" the knight asked the prior when the tumult had lessened enough for him to speak.

"We traveled at night," Prior Hugh said.

"Well, why not go back that way?"

"I don't think our companions would wish to do that. Ah," Prior Hugh said. At last he caught sight of Stephen and Gilbert. "Here they are now. Sir Robert, may I present Sir Stephen Attebrook and his companion, Gilbert Wistwode."

r Sir Robert Broun was a short man who was thick without being fat. He wore a flat-topped hat and a heavy cloak with slits in the sides for his arms. He carried green gloves of supple leather and had red-painted boots that rose to his knees. He was obviously prosperous, but he could have been a merchant except for the sword that hung at his side and the fine stallion held by the armed sergeant at his back.

Broun's eyes measured Stephen, who was rather less expensively dressed and acutely aware of the hole in his hose at the knee. Broun's face seemed perpetually fixed in a scowl. He noted the unstrung bow and case of arrows hanging from the pommel of Stephen's saddle and the stallion and second mare on leading reins, the mare laden with a shield and lance. He nodded as if satisfied that, although Stephen wasn't a wealthy knight, he at least was a fighting man. "Good day to you, sir."

"Expecting trouble?" Stephen asked.

"It is always wise to be cautious," Broun said as if he thought he had been rebuked.

Stephen nodded. "I would do the same, especially if I had my family in tow."

"Quite so," Broun said. "It's late. Let's be off. I have a long way to go and I do not wish to waste any more time."

The traveling party ambled against the current of people coming into town, crossed through Corve Gate and continued north up Corve Street. As they came abreast of a house owned by a widow named Helen Webbere, where a harmless and loyal little man had died last month in the alley beside it, Gilbert offered his mule to Prior Hugh.

"No, thank you, my son," Hugh said stiffly.

"Are you sure?" Gilbert said. "I don't mind walking."

"Nor do I." Hugh glanced at the mule without turning his head, as if he did not want anyone to think he was examining it.

Stephen smiled, wondering whether Gilbert's offer would have been rejected if the mule had been a horse. Like most churchmen in positions of authority, Hugh came from a gentry, perhaps even a baronial, family, if his accent was any indication, and for such men to ride a mule was more demeaning than walking. A monk was supposed to set aside earthy pride and earthly impulses in the service of God, but even the best men found that hard to do.

Within a few minutes, the houses gave way to pasture and field on each side of the road, except for the solitary thatched roof of an inn at the junction of the Linney path coming in from the left. A hundred yards beyond that, the road turned sharply left and crossed the River Corve, which was hardly more than a stream that ran clear over the rocks and weeds along its bottom. From the wooden bridge, Stephen even spotted the flash of a pair of sticklebacks, which scattered at the impact of a stone thrown by boys on the bank.

The casual traveler might be forgiven for thinking that he was still in the precincts of the town while south of the Corve, but on its north side there was no hiding the fact that the party had entered the country. More fields lay on either side of the road for a short distance, one of them plowed up for winter wheat and the other dotted with sheep grazing on stubble, but ahead loomed the forest that still covered much of England, dense and slightly forbidding, the leafless branches melancholy in the gray morning light.

Now that they had cleared the town and traffic dwindled, one might have expected the pace to quicken, but none of the folk on foot seemed interested in exerting themselves, in large part due to the number of children in the party, to the annoyance of Broun, who shot glances back at them from his place in the lead. But he said nothing to urge them on, although it was clear from his expression that he would have liked to do so. Nor did he quicken his own pace. The truth was, he benefited from their company as much as they from his, and that benefit would be lost if the party straggled and broke up.

To Stephen, it seemed as if he had spent more time traveling down one road or another than any other activity in his life, and since there were plenty of eyes to watch for trouble — not that he expected any, despite the rumors — he tied off the leading rein for the second mare and stallion, lay the reins of his mount against the pommel of his saddle and closed his eyes. He had slept on horseback many times in the past, so he was not afraid of falling off. The only hazard was that the mare would swerve to the verge of the road for a tuft of grass growing there, as she had a habit of doing if he did not keep an eye on her, and he might be left behind. But in the center of the road, with another horse to follow and surrounded by folk on foot, that did not seem to be a great risk.

He awoke to the drum of hoofs on the wooden bridge over the River Onny at Bromfield. The people on foot wanted to rest, and Broun at first ignored their cries. But when people just sat down, he reined his horse and waited, lips pressed together, while his wife, though pretending not to notice the delay, looked disgusted. The mason's wife removed a stone from her shoe and massaged her bare foot. The archers lay on their backs and one of them began to snore. A fight broke out among the players as to who would now have the right to ride in their wagon. There was only room for two in addition to the driver, so this was a matter of considerable importance, since the walk from the Corve had not cured their hangovers. The archers broke up the fight at Broun's insistence, and he ordered them all to walk as punishment. The order was ignored as soon as he had returned to the head of the line and the party resumed its march.

Onibury was only two miles beyond Bromfield, but it took them almost an hour to reach it. The people on foot wanted to use the occasion to declare another halt, but this time Broun was more firm in ignoring their pleas. He just kept going, and since his group had the majority of swords, those who had dallied now had to run to catch up.

For some reason known only to the ancient travelers who had made the original path, the road had re-crossed the Onny at Onibury and now they were on its eastern bank. The forest pressed in, with rising ground to the right of the road that rapidly grew steeper so that it shortly formed an embankment almost three times taller than a man.

The bramble on the slope was thick about the trunks of the oak and scattered pine. In summer, it would have concealed from sight anything on the slope and embankment, but now in November it was bare of leaves and afforded a view some distance in.

Still, the place worried Stephen. A man could still lie concealed on that slope until they had passed by. He had never been a robber himself, but he had mounted a few ambushes in Spain. You blocked the road in front of the marching column and behind so that you had them in a sack and poured arrows into the confused mass before the charge with horse. A proper robbery would lack the charge, but not the arrows or the blockages. Stephen strung the bow and nocked an arrow, and held the mare so that the party flowed around him. The stallion pounded a fore hoof at the delay and shied from anyone who got close. The mason's wife shot Stephen a worried look and pulled her little son out of the way as far as she could manage while remaining in the road..

When the last of them — which meant the players' wagon — had gone by, Stephen followed some distance back, casting around on every side for signs of movement. It struck him that although Robert Broun was a knight, he might not be much of a soldier, because he had neglected the need for a rear guard. He wished now he had his hauberk on, but it was rolled up in a leather sack behind the saddle cantle.

Gilbert had seen Stephen falling back and he held the mule at the verge until Stephen caught up. "Did you see something?" he asked anxiously.

"I thought I might spot a deer," Stephen said, eyes on the woods above them.

"You did not," Gilbert said.

"You never know. Haven't you ever ridden up on one grazing by the road?"

"But we're at the rear. Sir Robert will have scared them off."

"That's what you get when you're in a hurry."

"He certainly seems to be," Gilbert agreed.

They came to a break in the trees that lined the road on the western side. It was a gap wide enough for a cart to pass through. Someone had cleared the land for a field down on the flat land by the stream, which this year had been left in grass and had not even been mowed for hay.

"That's odd," Gilbert said.

"What? That the farmer forgot he has a fortune in hay down there?"

"No, there is a cart in the river. I wonder what it's doing there."

Gilbert pointed to the left. The stream bent westward at this point and on the other side, just before the bend, a sandbar glowed whitely in the gray light. Stephen saw the cart now. It lay in the middle of the stream on its side by the bar, only its wheels showing above the surface.

"That's no place for a cart," he said.

"I should say so," Gilbert said.

Stephen halted. Now that he took the time, he could see the impressions in the grass where the cart had been driven across the field. There were several other trails through the grass made by people on foot as well.

"Someone drove it into the stream," Stephen said.

"I cannot imagine why anyone would do so," Gilbert said dryly.

"Not a person in his right mind," Stephen said. He turned the mare off the road.

"Stephen," Gilbert said, "we'll be left behind." The players' wagon and the players were disappearing up the road.

"They'll be fine without us."

"I wasn't thinking of them."

"I know."

At the gap, a splash of red and yellow caught Stephen's eye. Reds and yellows were not unusual colors in the autumn, but these were too bright to be natural. He dismounted and bent down. Under the leaves, his fingers brushed the fletchings of an arrow. The shaft itself was fully buried and only the last half inch of the fletch was visible. He drew out the shaft. It was not unusual to lose an arrow while hunting, buried in the leaves. Sometimes you found old lost arrows, the shafts moldy and the points rusty. But this arrow was fresh, as if it had just come from the quiver.

"My word, what's that doing there?" Gilbert asked.

"I think it may have something to do with the cart."

He slipped the arrow into his quiver and rode into the field. He followed the track of the wagon, and saw that people had crossed and recrossed the field, beating down the tall grass in a welter of places that made it hard to tell who was doing what or going where.

He became aware of humming to the right, and glancing in that direction, saw what at first might be mistaken for a series of whitish stones laid out by the edge of the stream.

"Over here," Stephen said, swerving toward the objects.

"Oh dear," Gilbert said when he drew up. "Those poor people."

For the objects were not stones, but corpses — five men, a woman and a child of about four. They were naked and lay side-by-side. The men had puncture wounds here and there which were rimmed with black, dried blood. All the men had suffered head wounds as well, some from an axe and others, it appeared, from a club. The woman had her throat cut. The child had no obvious marks on the front of his body. Flies swarmed about them.

Stephen dismounted and felt the foot of one of the dead men. He promptly let go of the foot, for the body was already crawling with maggots. "It's still rigid."

"Killed yesterday, I would think," Gilbert said, kneeling beside him. "Probably late in the day. They haven't begun to change color yet." He meant that their skin still retained that translucent color of a fairly fresh body. After a day or so, even in the cool weather they had been having, a body usually began to take on greenish-red appearance as decay advanced.

Stephen nodded. He glanced back across the field toward the road. The confusion in the grass now made some sense. "They weren't killed here, except for the woman. They were dragged here after death." He gestured toward the woman's body, the eyes staring at the leaden sky; they were not normal, those eyes, but filmy and curiously flattened as if they were sinking back into the head.

"It appears so," Gilbert murmured. Even he, who had seen so much death in so many forms as a coroner's clerk, was shocked.

Stephen stood up. Now that he was at the edge of the stream, he noted that the sand along the opposite bank was trampled by horses and men. The stream made a broad curl here, approaching then receding from the road, and in the crook on the other side was a stand of forest. He gestured toward the forest. "They hid their horses there." He pointed to back toward the road. "They concealed themselves on the top of the embankment and shot these wretches as they happened by. No bothering with niceties, no stand and deliver. It was plain, flat murder." He took a few steps, turning as he went. "They spared the woman and child in the volley. Perhaps they fled through this field. I imagine a few of the killers remained with the horses and caught them trying to cross the stream."

Gilbert examined one of the wounds more closely. "These could have been made by arrows. But where are the arrows?"

"Pulled out, obviously. Why leave a good arrow behind? Arrows are expensive."

"So they are, so they are. But they missed one. You have it."

"Apparently so."

Gilbert gingerly turned over the child's body. The back was a welter of blue and red. The hair at the back of his head was matted and crusty with blood where he had been struck his death blow. Gilbert let the little body settle back. "A terrible thing to murder a child."

"He's old enough to tell what he had seen."

"Now what?" Gilbert asked, slipping his hands into his sleeves. He already knew what they had to do, of course; the question seemed more a courtesy, to allow Stephen to appear to make the decision.

Stephen sighed. "One of us will have to summon the hundred bailiff and the coroner for these parts. The other . . ." His voice trailed off.

"I will remain," Gilbert said. One of them had to; they were the first finders, and the law required the first finder to remain with the dead, if that were possible.

It would be a sad, gruesome duty, guarding the dead on this warming, quiet morning.

"I'll stay," Stephen said.

"You're sure?" Gilbert asked, trying not to display his relief.

"I imagine it's safe enough for the likes of you on the road. Whoever did this is twenty miles away by now."

"I should hope so. I would be, if it were me." Gilbert strode toward his mule.

"Catch up with the good prior and tell him that we've been detained," Stephen said. "Then go on to Stokesay. We can't be more than a mile from there. Have the lord send a messenger for the bailiff and coroner. It will save you a long ride." Stokesay was a manor that lay a short way off the road a little distance north of their location.

Gilbert mounted the mule as gracefully as a full barrel of ale being heaved into a cart. "So kind of you to think of my welfare at such a moment."

"I was thinking of the mule."

"Yes." Gilbert patted the mule's neck with a gesture meant to be affectionate, but somehow not quite managing it. "His back must hurt so now, carrying as great a burden as me for such a long way already."

He turned the mule's head toward the break in the tree line through which they had come.

Wind stirred the grass. The flies hummed.

Chapter 4

Stephen had a habit of leaping to conclusions, which had got him in trouble in the past when he had mistaken murder for a drowning, and he had leaped to quite a few in the last few minutes. It seemed plausible that the men had been shot on the road and killed there, while the woman and boy had been caught in the field as they fled. But there was no way he could prove the murder had happened this way. The marks left by the attackers and the victims were too muddled and ambiguous for that.

But there was one guess he could verify.

He mounted the first mare and, leading the other horses, swung around the dead. He crossed the stream some thirty or so yards from the corpses at a point where the sandy bank on the opposite shore began. There were no prints here, no mussed grass.

He dismounted just within the wood and tied off the horses.

As he did so, he heard voices. They came from the north. He paused and, sure enough, a party of travelers was just passing by on the road. Someone was telling a bawdy story about a miller's daughter. No one glanced in Stephen's direction. The story teller finished the tale to volleys of laughter. The voices receded and it was still again, except for the wind and the humming of the flies.

Eyes on the ground, he walked the edge of the wood as it ran beside the stream. Just beyond where the sandy bank emerged, he encountered a swath of churned up leaves about thirty feet wide where men and horses had moved back and forth. That swath led like a path to the overturned cart.

Stephen followed the swath into the wood for a short distance. The odor of horse manure hung in the air, and there were piles of manure running in a line parallel to the stream where the robbers had tethered a horse line. He counted the piles — fourteen — and was shocked at the answer. Fourteen horses was more a raiding party than a band of thieves and robbers.

Among the piles there was a small one of what appeared to be white sand. Stephen moistened a finger, dipped it in the white pile, and tasted the finger: salt. The remains of a small keg lay about the pile. It had been made of new, yellow wood, the slats snapped and broken as if a horse had stepped on it. Stephen fingered the slats of wood that had been the keg. An owner's mark had been burned across two of them. He put the slats together so he could see the mark in full: a dandelion with a drooping flower. He slid the slats with the mark into his belt.

All about the horse line, the leaves were churned up, evidence that there had been a great deal of moving about here. He walked in a circle around that area until, well within the wood, he crossed one, then another line of disturbance.

He trailed one line through the wood to the field on the far side. Hoof marks on some bare ground told him it was the path the robbers had taken when they arrived. It came from the southwest. Stephen continued to the other line of tracks, which showed that the robbers had departed due west.

Stephen put his dagger on the ground by the line of hoof prints, and paced off four steps and stopped. He lay down his sword, went back to the dagger and began counting hoof prints in the interval between the sword and the dagger, about ten feet of ground. The prints overlay each other so that most people would have no idea how many horses had passed this way. But the rear foot of a walking horse always lands on the space vacated by its front foot, leaving two distinctive half-moon marks that seem joined to each other, like strokes in a letter of an unknown alphabet. By counting those marks within the space he had defined, Stephen could get a good idea how many horses had been in the robbers' party. The count confirmed the impression he had gained from the piles of manure at the horse line.

He retrieved his weapons and the horses, and recrossed the stream. A decent distance from the corpses, he removed the bundle of clothing and gear from the second mare and tethered the horses by lengths of rope to the bundle, and allowed them to graze, while he sat down in the grass to think.

He let his mind go still so that his thoughts wandered this way and that without direction. Useful thoughts sometimes emerged by themselves out of the mire. Inevitably, his mind strayed to the victims' horror: walking along a country road, content with the companionship of your friends, looking forward to the end of the day and a hot meal; the abrupt shower of arrows, you and your friends pierced, the pain, trying to run, falling, a dark shape looming over you; the blur of the axe descending; and the final darkness.

Presently, he remembered something he had neglected to do.

Stephen rose and walked back to the road. At the gap, he studied the ground, looking for wheel marks. Many feet had come through this gap and the ground was hard here, so it was not easy to find the track. But it seemed to Stephen to curve to the north. That meant that the robbers had attacked to the north of the gap.

He walked north along the western edge of the road, scanning the ground and the foliage beside the road. At last, he came to a place where broken twigs on the foliage suggested that someone had force their way through.

Too much traffic had passed on the road to tell where the victims' wagon had been, but, glancing back to the gap where he had found the arrow, Stephen was convinced he had located the spot where the people had died. Arrows only buried themselves under leaves when shot at a flat trajectory. So now in his mind, he saw it: The attack had happened about here. The woman and child had taken shelter behind the wagon. When the robbers came down from the embankment, she had run. One of the robbers had shot at her from the road and missed, the arrow flying toward the gap and burying itself in the leaves. Oddly there was no evidence that anyone had followed the woman through the foliage. Someone waiting on the other side must have caught her, confirming his original suspicion.

To solidify this guess, Stephen climbed the embankment. It was hard going with his bad foot, for he had no toes on it to grip the slope. But at last, he reached the top.

And there, among the dense brush, he saw them – the impressions left by at least eight bodies lying on the ground.

Stephen searched the impressions in the hope that one of the attackers dropped some small article that might be used to identify him. But he found nothing.

There was nothing more he could do now but descend to the road and wait.

"It was not a mile to Stokesay," Gilbert said when he arrived more than two hours later. "It was more like two. That means I have gone four additional, unnecessary miles."

"It's too bad that you are not paid by the mile," Stephen said, rising from his seat against the embankment. "This adventure might make you rich."

"It would be a wonder if I am paid at all," Gilbert grumbled, and realizing that he had criticized Sir Geoff in front of strangers, he swung around and gestured to the rider and the wagon that followed him. By way of introduction he said, "This is Sir Thomas Perott."

"The coroner?" Stephen asked.

"No," Perott said. "Lord of Stokesay. This is my land. Where are they?"

Stephen pointed down the road. "In the field, there. You can get to it by that gap in the trees."

"I know it," Perott said. He barked orders to the men with the wagon, two of whom were the mason and the carpenter from the traveling party.

They waved to Stephen as they went by, but otherwise seemed grim enough to suit the occasion.

Perott got off his horse and handed the reins to the boy who rode with him. "What happened?" he asked.

Stephen briefly described what he had concluded about the attack.

Perott scuffed the ground. "Bad business," he said, obviously distressed that the robbery and murder had happened on land for which he was responsible. "Very bad business, indeed."

It occurred to Stephen that there might be adverse repercussions for Perott. There was a standing royal order that the roads were to be cleared for some distance on either side to frustrate, if not prevent, such robberies. If Perott really held this land, he had neglected that duty here, and he might have to answer for it before the sheriff. That might involve a fine.

They walked down to the gap and entered the field, where the men were piling the dead into the wagon.

"Master Gilbert tells me that you are a deputy coroner," Perott said.

"I am," Stephen answered.

Perott nodded. A brief tightening of his lips suggested that he did not like hearing the news confirmed.

When all the bodies were aboard the wagon, and the driver began to struggle out of the field, Perott said, "Well, you can at least come up to my house and stay the night. It's getting too late to press on with your journey. Besides, your monks are waiting for you there."

"I suspect their feet are sore, if my backside is any indication, my lord," Gilbert said. "I should like nothing better than to give it a rest."

"I should be happy if you would stay with us," Perott said in a grating tone that implied he was not happy at all, but politeness demanded that he make the offer.

Stokesay lay on the west side of the Onny away from the main road. The track to the manor house, for it really wasn't a castle, passed by a small stone church to the north. Men were already digging a large pit in the graveyard.

The driver took the wagon into the graveyard and stopped by the pit.

"Is it deep enough?" Perott asked one of the workmen.

"Aye, sir. It will do well enough."

"Let's get them planted before they start to stink."

"Should I fetch the chaplain, sir?"

"Yes, yes, let's get this done." Perott said to Stephen: "We don't have to stay for this."

"If it's all the same to you, sir, I shall, for the moment," Stephen said.

"Suit yourself." Perott turned his horse and trotted out of the graveyard, nodding to the chaplain emerging from the little church.

"What's the matter with him?" Gilbert asked as he and Stephen dismounted.

"He's unhappy."

"I can see that," Gilbert said. "I'm not blind. He has been in a panic since I first brought the news."

"Be glad that he's volunteered to feed you."

"Yes, but will it be slops?"

"Drop Sir Geoff's name a few times. He won't want to offend Sir Geoff."

"He doesn't seem to want to hear from me much. You drop it."

"What do you think I am, a courtier?"

"You could do with a little polish. Whatever Valence might have given you seems to have rubbed off."

Stephen grinned. "Too much time spent living with soldiers. You know what they're like."

"Cut above bandits, most of them," Gilbert grumbled.

The workmen finished unloading the bodies, which they dumped without ceremony in the pit, one on top of the other. The casual way they tossed in the dead troubled Stephen, but he had no say in how they were buried. The workmen shoved dirt over the corpses. With so many shovels, it did not take long to fill the hole.

The chaplain muttered a few prayers in Latin.

Everyone turned away. It was supper time, after all, and the men were hungry.

"That's that, I suppose," Gilbert said. "We should be grateful that Perott at least buried them in consecrated ground."

"I wonder who they were," Stephen said.

"Not likely that we'll ever know."

"I guess not. Well, let's hope that we aren't late for supper. I doubt Perott will feel inclined to save anything for the likes of you."

Set within a palisade, the manor house was a timber-framed building abutting a stone tower on its north side which was not any taller than the peak of the house roof and lacked crenellations, a sign that it was unlicensed. It was much like the house in which Stephen had grown up. Such house-tower homes were not uncommon in this part of England. The towers were refuges against raiders. Otherwise, they were mainly used for storage, since few people liked to live in them, for they were cramped and badly heated in winter.

As he rode through the gate, he was surprised to see a second tower under construction on the south side of the hall. Its walls stood only as high as man's head, however, and work had halted, owning to the onset of autumn. Mortar would not set during this time of year and building would not pick up until spring. But the partly built tower explained the presence of the mason and carpenter: they had come looking for work.

Supper was a somber affair. It was a light meal of cold fish, cheeses and dried fruit left over from dinner. Perott's wife made a heroic effort to keep the conversation going, but the host responded in grunts to any overture. Stephen did his best to participate but he was not naturally deft or witty, nor was he interested, for he could not put behind him what he had seen that day. So the main players were Prior Hugh and Gilbert, who never lacked for words in any situation and was almost as good a source of news as Harry the beggar.

When the tables had been taken down and the benches cleared away, Perott and his guests settled around the octagonal stone hearth in the center of the floor. This was an old house and had no chimneys; indeed, many houses were still built without them. They were expensive and few wanted the cost of such a fashionable frivolity except in a kitchen. Servants poured wine and heaped wood on the fire until it was a happy blaze and there was warmth at least in the middle of the cavernous dark space.

"I suppose," Perott said, "you will be going on in the morning."

"We should wait for the coroner or his deputy," Stephen said. "And the jury."

Prior Hugh, on the other side of the fire, did not look pleased at this proposal. He had obviously hoped to be back in his priory by now. Perhaps he worried that it would be leaking monks while he was away or at least suspected murderers who now might not be caught. But he made no immediate objection.

"I don't see why," Perott said.

"To give my testimony," Stephen said. "I am the first finder." He glanced at Gilbert. "One of them, at any rate."

"We shall go tonight," Prior Hugh said. "Clun isn't but ten miles from here by road. We shall be there before dawn. And the lands around Clun are safer than here."

"We are safe enough," Perott said, irritated.

"This is the fourth such murder along the Shrewsbury road in a month," Hugh snapped, who now showed himself more informed that he had revealed at supper. "At least the lord of Clun knows how to protect his lands and keep people safe."

"I keep my people safe!" Perott snapped, fairly shouting.

"Your people, perhaps," Hugh said, "but what of those innocent travelers?"

"I cannot have a watch everywhere," Perott said. "It is a long road."

"I appreciate your hospitality," Hugh said, standing. "But we will not need beds tonight after all."

"Suit yourself," Perott said. Then he added, as if a thought had just occurred to him. "I see you are concerned about traveling without your companions. There is a way they can be free to accompany you in the morning."

"Indeed?" Hugh asked. "How?"

"My clerk can take down their testimony," Perott said, gesturing to Stephen and Gilbert. "I will present the writing when the coroner arrives. It could be days, even weeks before they get here. It is a long way to Shrewsbury."

"It should be only twenty miles," Stephen said.

"A day for my messenger to get there," Perott answered. "Several days for the coroner to stir himself from his brew, and a day to get back. Before you know it a week has passed."

"A week," Hugh murmured, dismayed.

"Is this done?" Stephen asked Gilbert.

Gilbert steepled his hands. "Yes, in rare cases."

Perott thumped the arm of his chair. "There! You can do your duty to the dead and to the prior at the same time. Look at how unhappy this affair has made him. He would risk a night journey for the urgency of his mission. Aren't you here to protect him from the perils of the road?"

"Partly," Stephen said.

"You could really just give a writing?" Hugh asked, visibly anxious about avoiding a walk through the night.

"It has been done," Gilbert repeated.

"Then why not?" Hugh asked.

Stephen did not answer the prior. Apprehension pricked at his mind: a suspicion of something not done. He said to Perott instead: "You haven't sent the messenger yet."

"Well, no," Perott said.

"Why not?"

"I wanted to see for myself what the mischief was." He added defensively, "I am short handed here. I cannot afford to send off someone on a lark."

"It is hardly a lark," Stephen said. "It is slaughter, plain and simple."

"I have seen that now," Perott said.

"So you have. And it is still early. The men who did this left evidence of their passing. If we act quickly, they could yet be caught."

"I am doing what duty requires," Perott said.

"What will you do, Sir Stephen?" Hugh asked, clearly wanting an answer.

Stephen paused, thinking about where his duty lay. He had not been sent to investigate the murder of the travelers, but on an altogether different chore. Which had priority? The unknown dead, Sir Geoff . . . or Christopher, his son?

He said, "Send for your clerk."

Chapter 5

Stokesay hall was spacious, but it had no separate accommodations for visitors, so the travelers slept in a corner of the great hall with the servants. The only concession was that they had feather mattresses, while the servants had hay. The lack of a separate room was not so great a hardship, however, since a sleepless someone kept the fire going throughout the night.

It had burned down to embers again when Stephen awoke just before dawn to the sound of the cook and his helpers dressing, rolling up their beds and stacking them in a corner, leaving for the kitchen.

On the way out, a cook's helpers kicked one of those who remained in bed.

"Leave off!" grumbled the object of this attention.

"They want to leave early, remember? Get up!"

The man who had been kicked did not arise for some moments. Presently he got up and began to dress — like most people he slept naked. An elderly man with a beard that hung to his chest, he was not a pretty sight in the faint glow of the fire: all spindly legs and sagging belly. He left the hall just as others began sitting up, still huddled under their blankets as if savoring that last moments of rest.

Stephen threw off his blankets, pulled on his boots — he had slept fully clothed — and went out into the yard. By the time he emerged, the cook had the shutters on the kitchen open and the boys were encouraging the fire with a bellows as if it were a forge. The cook spotted him and laid a quarter of a loaf of bread and a chunk of dry cheese on the ledge.

"This will get you started, sir," the cook said.

The door to the stables was open and Stephen entered. The old man, who was a groom, had Stephen's horses and the mule tethered to rings outside their stalls and was saddling them.

"I expect you'll be busy this morning," Stephen said.

"Busy enough, sir," the groom said.

"You've got no help?"

"My boy's got a flux."

"Who will be going to Shrewsbury?"

"Shrewsbury? Why, no one."

"No one?"

"Not that I've been told."

"But those people . . ."

"Those people? You mean the folk murdered?"

"No one's going to take word about them?"

"Not that anyone's told me." He finished with a pack saddle and started on the mare that Stephen would ride.

"I'm sure that we'll have the undersheriff down here asking about them before long," the groom said. "You're going to Clun, though, aren't you?"

"Right."

"That's a safe road, once you get away from the highway. Everybody says so. Don't worry yourself, or that little prior. You'll be fine."

"That is odd," Gilbert said when Stephen told him about the conversation with the groom. "I would think that fellow would know. But perhaps Perott or the steward had not spoken to him about it."

The three monks were walking forty yards ahead, striding down the highway as if they were in a hurry to get quickly to their destination. Stephen had his bow strung and an arrow nocked even though the land here was clear on both sides of the road: a great broad field to the left belonging to Stokesay and a lesser field to the right that quickly gave way to a wooded hill. He also had put on his hauberk and gambeson. Perhaps armor would not truly make him safer from a surprise attack, but it made him feel that way and had seemed to give Prior Hugh and his companions some comfort.

"It takes a full day to get to Shrewsbury," Stephen said. "I'd think anyone going there would want to get an early start."

"Well, I agree. I would if it were me."

"Naturally. You might even want two days for the journey."

"I would not!"

"Well, I'm sure it would take that long, given your penchant for stops to ease your backside."

"My backside may not be as tough as yours, but it is tough enough. I managed to make it into deepest Wales well enough once."

"As you repeatedly assure me. But there is still much room for improvement."

"I shall watch you closely, as you clearly think you are a model to emulate."

"You could do worse," Stephen said with some false bravado, remembering the odd looks he had generated when he mounted his horse from the right earlier that morning rather than from the customary left — "Don't mind him. He is eccentric," Gilbert had murmured to the old groom who had openly gaped in amazement as if some sin had been committed. Since Stephen had lost part of his left foot, he was certainly no model to emulate. That foot could not use a stirrup and hung against the mare as if he were riding bareback. Gilbert would have enough trouble even if he were tied to a saddle; bareback he could never manage.

"At this rate, we shall be in Clun by dinner time," Gilbert said, preferring to avoid the subject of horses and address the subject of food. He had an appetite that would have done for at least two men, maybe more.

"Looking forward to the pleasures of a priory's table, are you?"

"They often do tend to eat well. After the breakfast we received, I should think you would be too."

"The lord of Stokesay did seem very anxious to be rid of us."

"And he sends no messenger to Shrewsbury," Gilbert mused.

"As if he wanted the dead to remain unknown and unremarked."

"I thought that dumping them into a common pit was unfeeling." Gilbert swayed along on his mule, clutching the pommel for balance. "You don't think he might have had anything to do with their deaths, do you?"

"The thought occurred to me."

"If I was a lord who found it profitable to prey upon travelers, I would not murder them in my own lands."

"You might if you wanted to allay suspicions."

"Perhaps, I suppose. But that seems reckless."

"True, but men who are desperate enough to turn to robbery and murder do not always think things through. They are prone to mistakes."

"Ah, yes, no doubt in your former life you had acquaintance with such men."

"A few."

Gilbert sighed. "I have lived a cloistered life, I'm afraid. I have seen much suffering but I cannot imagine men who would slaughter such simple people just for their trifles. But tell me this — if this was a cunning act to put the authorities off the trail, why would I bury the dead and tell no one if for no other reason but to bury the crime as well?"

"All right. Let us suppose Perott is not a murderer. Why else would he hurry us on our way, and apparently has no intention of reporting this crime?"

"Consider this. Remember that the road had not been cleared?"

"Yes, I remember. You think he's worried about that? It is a small fine."

"But he is also building a second tower. I'll bet the sheriff doesn't know about that. Any visitor from Shrewsbury is bound to mention it. Fines for unlicensed towers and castles tend to be more substantial than for the failure to cut bushes."

"As are the licenses themselves," Stephen agreed.

"Perhaps Perott wishes to avoid all those expenses. Towers are costly enough and he does not hold a great deal of land. His income may not be up to all the costs. Whatever his intentions, no one will investigate the circumstances of the deaths of those poor people. It is a shame."

"At least not yet," Stephen said.

Ahead, a road was just coming into view on the left. The junction sat in a patch of woods, unmarked, and unattended by any houses. The monks took the road without a glance back.

"Ah," Gilbert said, standing in his stirrups to stretch and teetering so that Stephen almost reached out to steady him. "The Clun road. It's not far now. A mere nine more miles."

The road climbed toward Wales, and within an hour they reached the village and manor of Aston-on-Clun, where they met the River Clun. Stephen expected the monks to halt for a rest and for water, but Prior Hugh passed through the village without stopping. Stephen watered the animals at the village well, which allowed Gilbert to stretch his legs, and they caught up with the monks a few hundred yards down the road. Hugh wore a thunderous expression of impatience as they drew up, but at the sight of Stephen and Gilbert, he marched up the road without any reproof they could hear.

"He seems to be in quite a hurry," Gilbert remarked.

"Perhaps he doesn't want to be late for dinner," Stephen said. "At this pace we should reach Clun before noon."

"Yes," Gilbert said, not enthusiastic about two more nonstop hours in the saddle. "I hope I am well fed for this suffering."

"I doubt he cares much about the state of your backside or your stomach."

"Sadly, I am sure that is true."

On either side, the hills grew taller as they advanced and in many places the forests on the crests crept down to engulf the road. Long stretches seemed wild and uninhabited, the perfect haunt for robbers.

At last, they broke out of the forest into a broad field that on the right ran up a gentle slope and on the other lay flat along the river. Ahead in the distance, the peaks of roofs could be seen, and over them projected the finger of a stone tower that had to belong to Clun castle.

"Ah," Gilbert said, "we have arrived."

He seemed to think that this entitled him to dismount and rest his bottom and stretch his legs. But as his feet hit the ground, Hugh picked up his pace as if the road burned his feet and he was ever more anxious to be off it. In moments, the distance between the monks and Stephen and Gilbert grew from a mere thirty yards to fifty or more and expanding.

"I wonder what's got into him?" Gilbert said as he waddled after the monks.

"As anxious for dinner as you, I suppose," Stephen said. "Am I going to get to see you run now? That's always amusing."

Gilbert scowled and slowed down. "I have never been to Clun. If we lose sight of him, we shall have to find the priory ourselves."

"I think that the locals will know where it is."

Ahead, where a tree line marked one field off from its neighbor, a dozen horsemen armed with hunting spears and crossbows appeared, trotting toward the road. Suddenly, they spurred to a gallop and within moments had reached the road and surrounded the three monks.

The sound of voices raised in anger reached Stephen. He frowned. "I don't like the looks of that."

"Not robbers surely," Gilbert said. "Not this close to Clun."

"I don't think so, but trouble of some sort," Stephen said, fumbling with the straps that bound his shield to the second mare. He hung the shield to his shoulder and spurred the first mare to a canter.

He could no longer see the monks, who were surrounded by a solid wall of horses and mounted men. Many of the spears dipped toward the monks within the circle of horses, and Stephen's mouth went dry at the thought the monks were being attacked — a possibility that seemed beyond belief.

The mounted men were so intent on the monks that no one gave Stephen any notice until he had reached them and said, "Prior Hugh! I'm sorry! We were detained!"

Heads swung in Stephen's direction and the leveled spears swung skyward, making a thicket about Prior Hugh and a man with the great shoulders of a bear, who bore no spear himself, but had a crossbow on his back. He wore a rich display of colors: cloak, tunic with billowing sleeves and hose an array of reds, blues, and gold. Leather boots painted purple rose to his knees and a gold broach fastened the cloak at his neck. He was about forty, with a great head of close-cropped reddish hair that perched like a boulder on those massive shoulders. His thick wrists were banded with silver bracelets that, though broad, seemed small and delicate, as did his legs, seemingly too thin to support so great a frame. His eyes, narrowed in anger, seemed almost to disappear as his scowl deepened.

"Who are you?" he asked Stephen.

"I am Stephen Attebrook."

The scowl lessened and a certain wariness crept into the man's face. "Of the Shelburgh Attebrooks?"

"A cousin."

"Eustace has many cousins. Which one are you?"

"I am the one who went to Spain."

The light of understanding peeped through the scowl. "You're the one sent to London to become a lawyer," the big man said with a sneer, "who ran away."

"I seem to be famous for that, I am afraid. I have always preferred a sword to a pen and Master Valence could not beat the love of pens into me. Now, courtesy demands that I ask you the same question: Who are you?"

"I am Percival FitzAllan, and this is my land you're standing on. What is your business here?"

"My lord," Stephen said, "I felt an urge to pray at St. George's Priory."

"What for? It is a pile of horse shit, a reek of hovels around a mound of stone that pretends to be a church. Nobody goes there."

"My friend the prior assured me it was a fine establishment and that I could find peace for my soul there."

"Your friend the prior?" FitzAllan spat.

"Yes. He needed protection, for the Shrewsbury road is plagued with robbers, as we saw for ourselves, to our dismay, when we found a family of merchants who had been murdered and their wares plundered just north of Onibury. A vicious band, too — they even killed a child."

"Murdered, you say." FitzAllan shot a glare at one of the mounted men armed with a crossbow.

"Shot down on the road and axed and beaten where they lay."

"A nasty bit of business. I've heard there have been troubles hereabout. So, you thought to visit the priory, then?"

"I had nothing to do, so I thought I would see this part of the country and pay my respects to God."

"And how did you meet the good prior? He hides in his pile of shit like a rabbit in his hutch. This is the first time I've seen him abroad in many weeks." FitzAllan turned to the prior, who was forcing his way through the circle of horses. "What are you doing on my land? I warned you!"

"He is on the high road," Stephen said. "He has a right to be here just like anyone else."

"Out here," FitzAllan said with menace, "in the March — on my land — I decide the rights of men. If I don't like them, they do not trespass. Sometimes they do not even live."

"Yes, I see that you don't like Prior Hugh. But he is with me, and he will pass on the road as he wills."

FitzAllan's face went red. He breathed heavily, like an ox considering a charge.

For a moment, Stephen feared that he had made a mistake and that FitzAllan would order his men to attack. Stephen could not fight a dozen men by himself. But boldness and bluff had seemed the only thing to do.

"There is a toll," FitzAllan said. "You have not paid it."

"The toll does not apply until you pass through the town," Prior Hugh said.

"The toll applies when I say it does," FitzAllan said.

"I heard you give the ruling at one of your own courts," Hugh said. "I remember quite distinctly. Yet I know it is your pleasure to change the law at whim. You may do so and apply it to me, but would you be so contrary to a man of good family as Sir Stephen? That would be unnecessarily rude." He dug in his purse for a half-penny, which he tossed to one of FitzAllan's men. "This is for your toll."

FitzAllan's face went even redder. Then the color subsided almost to normal. He turned his horse's head. "Enjoy your prayers!" he called over his shoulder as dug in his heels. "They'll keep you awake all night with their singing! When you're tired of it, come visit me and I'll show you how men live!"

The other horsemen clattered after their lord. In the distance, Stephen could hear a pack of hounds barking.

"Having trouble with your neighbor, are you?" Stephen said to Prior Hugh.

"He is a bastard," Hugh said. He turned and marched up the road toward Clun.

"I thought monks were supposed to maintain a mild temper," Stephen said to Gilbert who had finally reached them.

"He seems to be put out, I must say," Gilbert said.

"In a most unmonklike way."

The town of Clun was big and wealthy enough to have its own wall, but not so wealthy that the burghers could afford a stone one. They had settled for a heaped up embankment of earth with a wooden palisade on top. Stephen expected to have to pass through the town and was steeling himself to pay the toll when, fifty yards shy of the gate, the monks took a lane that led south to the river. Prior Hugh halted at a ford so that the other two monks could hoist him on their shoulders. His bearers splashed into the river, which was really no more than a stream here and ankle deep. They set him on the ground on the opposite bank, and without a look back, headed up the lane. Beyond, up a gentle hill, a stone building reared behind some leafless trees.

"That must be it," Gilbert said with obvious relief, urging his mule into the water. The mule paused in midstream for a drink and only continued when Stephen gave him a slap on the rump that caused him to start.

"Careful, there!" Gilbert said, clutching the mule's mane.

"You could use a bath. I don't think Clun is large enough to support a bath house."

"I prefer not to appear as a wet rag when we pay our first respects at the Augustine Priory of St. George, if it's all the same to you."

The lane wound up the hill, bordered by tall hedges. Almost at the top was a fork, with a path leading off to the south. The lane curved to the right and within a few steps they had arrived.

"Oh my," Gilbert sighed. "It is not quite what I had expected. Not nearly so grand."

"Not grand at all," Stephen said.

The main buildings of the priory were laid out in the customary square with the church forming the northern side. During the approach, it had looked more like a barn than a church. But as Stephen dismounted by the gate leading to the cloister, he saw that the stone building was intended to be a church and it was unfinished. The northern and eastern walls seemed complete, but the west, which should have contained the entrance, and the south were only a third built and the whole had no roof except for a portion above the eastern end, where the altar was located. He would have expected to see signs of construction on such an important building, but there was no scaffolding in evidence and moss grew on the tops of exposed stone, showing that no one had worked on the church in some time. The remaining buildings forming the square were wattle and timber, thatched rather than built in stone and topped with slate or clay tiles. Across the road stood a tight cluster of other buildings belonging to the priory: a smithy, granary and barn, a brew house, a pigsty, various sheds, a garden and orchard, and beyond them all a windmill.

He saw a flicker of movement at the west end of the church. At first he thought it was someone peeking out to see who had arrived. But when he looked in that direction, whatever had produced the flicker had disappeared. It probably was nothing but a bird.

"They seem to be rather poor monks," Stephen said.

"That is no crime," Gilbert said.

"I wonder if Sir Geoff has been here to see what the brothers have done with his wife's gift."

"I doubt it." Gilbert sighed again.

Hugh and his monk companions had gone through the gate into the cloister without a word to Stephen and Gilbert, who stood there wondering what to do for several moments. A man of perhaps sixty or so with a thick gray beard and long gray hair appeared, wiping the evidence of a meal from his beard with his hands, which he wiped on his shirt.

"Sirs!" he cried. "Your pardon! We are all at dinner! I am Anselm, the porter. Welcome to St. George's."

Chapter 6

The porter took Stephen's sword, which he put in some rooms to the right of the gate, and waited while Stephen pulled off his hauberk, rolled it up and returned to its leather bag. The porter led them through the gate, which ran like a tunnel through the building forming the western range of the priory. They crossed the cloister to the south range and he left them at the door.

"Eat hearty, fellows" he said with a chuckle that seemed more sarcastic than humorous, and he ducked away quickly when one of the brothers appeared in the doorway.

"Good morning," the monk said cheerfully. "I am Brother John. The prior has asked me to look after you." He was short, slender and very young, barely out of his teens, his narrow face scarred by smallpox. The hem of his robes was badly frayed and he had a hole at the end of his shoe that revealed his big toe. "We are almost finished with dinner, I'm afraid, but please come this way. I've asked the fraterer to provide for you."

"The fraterer?" Stephen murmured to Gilbert as they took their seats.

"The brother in charge of delivering the food and drink."

The servant led them toward a long table on the other side of the long narrow room. It was rather like the hall in any manorial dwelling with the tables arranged against the walls and a fire in a hearth on the floor in the middle. Though a large room, the mere dozen people present made it seem even greater in size. Stephen spotted Hugh in the center of a knot of monks by a door on the left, in deep and earnest conversation. Above the murmur of this conversation, a monk standing on a wooden pulpit read in Latin from a thick book.

A scarecrow of a monk came through the door at the west end of the refectory followed by two servants bearing wooden trays. He waved at the guests and the servants hurried over. They deposited bowls of clear soup, salted cod, a hard white cheese, bread rolls and a bowl of butter. One of them set down a jug of cider rather than the usual ale and two drinking bowls.

"Ah," Stephen said as the servants withdrew, "salted cod. My favorite."

"It is Wednesday after all," Gilbert said defensively: Wednesdays, Fridays and Saturdays where supposed to be meatless, according to church custom, although many nonreligious houses were not strict in their observance of this rule. "At least you have butter for your bread. Just remember not to wipe your mouth on the table cloth, if you can."

"May I use my sleeves instead?"

"No, you may not. And don't spit on the floor either."

"I will reserve my spit for our visit to FitzAllan."

"Your visit, perhaps, but not mine. I think I shall avoid him. He seemed like an unpleasant fellow."

"Yes, but our host has not been the model of geniality either."

Gilbert glanced at Hugh, who was still locked in conversation. "I wonder why."

There was a brief interruption when one of the monks rang a small bell and all the brothers present turned and prayed toward a painting of the cross on the eastern wall behind the high table. All the monks filed out of the refectory.

It did not take long to dispose of the meal put before them, and a servant, who had them under observation, swept away the bowls without delivering a second course. The refectory was now deserted, except for Gilbert and Stephen. A bell clanged beyond the door, only faintly audible so that Stephen wasn't sure at first that he heard it. But it sounded again, and Gilbert smiled, as if at a pleasant memory. He said: "Sext. It's time for Sext."

"What's that?" Stephen said.

"The noon service, of course."

Gilbert rose and went to the east door. He pointed a finger at the door and said, "The dormitory is through here. They are going to the church."

"Good for them," Stephen said, wishing that there had been more to the meal than watery soup, a few hard slabs of salted cod and some cheese that, he had discovered, had a bit of mold on it — and this for the main meal of the day; God knew what lay in store for supper. Burnt bread and water? He had the feeling that his stay at the priory would not be a pleasure romp. He had been looking forward to a soft bed and good food at least as partial payment for this journey, because he had always heard that monks lived well within their cloisters. If the outlook was for moldy cheese and a diet of salted cod, he was anxious to get his business here done as quickly as possible.

Gilbert looked as though he wanted to enter the dormitory and follow the monks. But that would have been rude. Instead, he went out to the cloister. Stephen would have preferred to pull a bench close to the fire on the hearth, but it was burning low and not providing much warmth. So he pulled his cloak about him and went out after Gilbert.

The cloister was nothing more than the square formed by the long rectangular buildings erected around it, and it was not large: Stephen could have thrown a stone across from the refectory and bounced it off the wall of the church.

Gilbert already stood under one of the windows of the church, which gazed down from above the timber awning that ran around the interior of the cloister. The singing had already begun when Stephen reached him. He didn't know what the song was, but the monks had a good collection of voices. Gilbert listened with his eyes closed and a pleasured smile, lips moving silently.

"They sing well," Stephen said.

"Hush!" Gilbert said and went back to mouthing the words. He wiped his eyes.

"What's the matter with him?" a very English voice said above their heads and to the left.

"Don't provoke him," Stephen said, catching sight of the speaker who proved to be a young blond man wearing a blue shirt and faded brown hose, perched in a window of the church. "He is a terror when he is angry."

"He doesn't look so terrible to me," the young man said. "He's just a silly little fat man."

"He can be, take my word for it," Stephen said moving beneath the young man. "Who are you? I thought only monks were allowed in the church during services."

"Well, as I live in the church at the moment, I'm allowed."

"You live in the church."

"That's what I said. Are you hard of hearing?"

"I heard what you said, and if you speak to me like that again, I'll come up there and break your head for your insolence."

The young man grinned, not the least bit intimidated. "Then you'll have the prior after you. I've got sanctuary here. No one can touch me. Not even Lord Percival."

Stephen wanted to ask the fellow what he meant by that, but he withdrew from the window before he had a chance.

The singing continued within the church. Gilbert was lost in his memories, eyes clamped shut. There was nothing for Stephen to do but wait, so he sank to a bench, plucked a stem of grass, and chewed on the end. Waiting was never something he did well, however. Soon he rose and paced the paths that crossed the interior of the cloister and along the walls beneath the wooden awning. Once in Spain, he had been in a similar cloister, for most were built on the same plan. It had been much larger and made of sculpted stone, roof and supports alike surrounding a splendid garden crossed by paved gravel walkways, and had presented a grand and impressive sight. The memory of that place, white stone ablaze in the sunlight, only made this cloister seem all the more shabby, with its gray unpainted wood and packed dirt beneath the awning. Sir Geoff would be appalled if he saw it.

Presently, the singing stopped. Stephen heard a faint voice speaking in Latin. Finally, the church was silent. Gilbert opened his eyes and wiped his face. He sank to a bench and heaved a sigh.

"All done?" Stephen asked.

Gilbert nodded.

"Feel better?"

Gilbert nodded again.

"You don't look better."

Gilbert shot him as hard a look as his round jovial face could manage.

The fat purse Sir Geoff had given Stephen for expenses weighed heavily in his leather belt bag. Dinner had been such a mean affair that Stephen's stomach still needed filling. Gilbert's stomach must be suffering even more than his own. He was about to suggest that they repair to the town, where there had to be a tavern, to throw away some of Sir Geoff's money on a bit of meat and ale, when that young monk Brother John appeared at a door into the east range. Brother John spotted them and came across the cloister. He said, "Sirs, Prior Hugh requests your presence."

"An audience with the prior," Stephen said, sorry at the interruption of his plan. "Not my idea of fun on a chilly afternoon."

"Don't be rude," Gilbert said.

"Why not?" Stephen asked. "He's not been the pinnacle of friendliness so far."

"He has many weighty matters on his mind," Gilbert said. "Doesn't he, brother?"

"Oh, yes," Brother John said. He gestured toward the east range. "This way."

"So you have met Oswic," Hugh said. His narrow face was drawn and tired. "He is a symptom of our troubles, not the source. How much did he tell you?"

"Getting conversation out of him was like trying to get a bird to talk," Stephen said. "He only sang the song that pleased him, much of it sharp."

Hugh sighed. "Yes. He can be dislikeable."

"Yet you protect him."

"I have no choice. He has claimed sanctuary in our church, and he is entitled to our protection, even if it is only half built," Hugh said. "Besides, I believe he can be redeemed. He can be a decent fellow when he wants to. He charmed a good girl into marriage over the objections of her father — had to charm the father too, from what I hear, as the boy is only a carter and the girl a tailor's daughter. And he has been a good husband to her, from all accounts." Hugh sighed. "I am glad of that. A fine girl, that one. She can even read and write a bit, since she does her father's accounts. Oswic claims that she has even taught him some letters and numbers. So perhaps we can find a way to make something of him."

"But the church is not consecrated as one yet," Gilbert said. "So the claim of sanctuary is technically wrong."

Hugh looked at him sharply. "It would be a church if FitzAllan had not interfered. And to me — to us — it is fully a church, and I shall treat it as such. A community such as ours cannot survive without a church. It is the center of our lives."

A gust of chill air blew against the half-open shutter and it banged against the wall of Hugh's room, which occupied a south corner of the long dormitory. He rose and closed the shutter, sending the room into semidarkness. To give them light, he lit a candle. It produced only a little ball of illumination, but that was sufficient for them to see each other's faces. The candle filled the room with the acrid scent of tallow.

Hugh no longer wore the same habit in which he had traveled to Ludlow. That one had been decently made and fairly new. This one was old, careworn and patched in many places.

Hugh sat down again on his cushioned chair. He said, "The existence of our community is threatened. If something is not done, and quickly, it will end." He steepled his fingers and gazed into a corner. "We were once a community of twenty-eight brothers. Now we are only fifteen. Some we have lost to natural death, but most have simply abandoned us. I fear that more will leave soon, now that winter is upon us." He added vehemently, "FitzAllan means to strangle us, to see the priory fail."

"Why?" Gilbert asked.

"Our land was once a manor belonging to the Fitz Warains. But FitzAllan had a claim to it as well. He went to law over it. The case dragged on for years. His last appeal failed four years ago. Since then he has not permitted us the liberty of passage on the road through his lands or those of any of his retainers, or access to the Clun market. In consequence the priory has been neither able to sell its produce nor to buy necessaries. We have no money nor the means to get any. Oh, we have a factor who trades some of our goods in Wales for us and brings back a few needful things. But the cost of that is steep and the returns few. Building on our church has stopped, and the brothers go without salt and other things that relieve the pangs of life."

He leaned forward, elbows on his knees. "For the first two years, the brothers endured this deprivation with admirable stoicism. But then, some started leaving. A drip here, a dribble there, one a month, perhaps two."

"Hardship is the lot of the monk, sacrifice and suffering are their robes," Gilbert said.

"They are supposed to be," Hugh said, "but not all brothers have the same capacity for sacrifice and endurance, I am afraid. The spirit may be strong enough, but the body is weak."

"You are not sharing this with us to make conversation," Stephen said.

"No," Hugh answered. "I wish you to better understand the urgency of your mission."

"Solving the riddle of a murder is always urgent," Stephen said.

"It is in its own right," Hugh hastened to add. "William's death has deeply frightened the brothers, and shaken their faith more than our deprivations have done. You must find the killer and point the finger of justice at him. It is the only way to save us."

"That will do nothing about FitzAllan," Gilbert said.

Hugh fixed him with a glare. "But it will. FitzAllan is the murderer."

The accusation hung in the air like its own foul smell.

"You have a witness," Stephen said.

"No."

"You have evidence, then."

"Yes, well, no. Not exactly."

"What have you got?"

"It can only be him," Hugh said with conviction.

"You have only your suspicions," Stephen said.

Hugh did not answer directly. He paused, as if gathering his thoughts. "That young fellow Oswic. He is one of FitzAllan's tenants, a quarrelsome lad, given to arguments and fights. Thursday last in Clun, he picked an argument with one of FitzAllan's archers, It came to daggers and the archer was slain. Oswic fled across the river out of FitzAllan's domain. He found the doors of the village church down the road locked, so he came here. With our church as it is, you can understand that he had no trouble getting in and reaching the altar.

"FitzAllan soon found out where Oswic was hiding, of course, and he led a party of armed men to arrest him. But the brothers made a palisade of their bodies and refused him admittance. FitzAllan is a hard ruthless man, but he is wary of antagonizing the Fitz Warains, who still have some interest in our priory, and he remembered the example of Beckett. So he stayed his hand and went away.

"Two days later, we found Brother William dead."

"That is not enough to accuse FitzAllan," Gilbert said.

"I know that!" Hugh snapped. "But it had to be him. It was a message, a grim and terrible message. He has lost patience with his plan to starve us out! Now he means to drive us out with fear, and to kill those who remain."

He slapped the arms of his chair. "You must find the proof of FitzAllan's guilt! It is the only way to save the priory!" He paused again, and added plaintively, "Please."

Brother John was waiting when they emerged from the prior's chamber. He sat on a monk's bed with folded hands and bowed head, still as a statue, and it appeared that he had not moved since he had fetched them to the prior an hour ago. He rose and said, "May I show you to the guest house? It's really not a house, just a set of rooms across the cloister in the west range where many of the lay brothers sleep. But we like to call it that. One day we will have a real guest house."

"What happened to Brother William's body?" Stephen asked grimly, brushing aside John's attempt at pleasantry.

John blinked. "Why, buried, of course."

"Of course," Gilbert murmured. "Where else would he be after so much time."

"Thank you, Gilbert," Stephen said. "Did you see the body?"

"Only when it had been prepared and laid by the high altar of the church when we said a mass for him," John said.

"Who found him?" Stephen asked.

"That would be Brother Simon."

"Where is he now?"

"Around somewhere. We both work for the cellarer. I am one of the chief assistants, after Brother William, of course. Brother William was the subcellarer, and when he did not appear for Prime, Brother Simon was sent to fetch him."

"And who prepared the body for burial?"

"Brother Odo."

"Is there anyone else who might have seen the body and any injuries it might have suffered?"

"Only the prior and the subprior. Simon went straight to the prior who would not let anyone else near."

"So only those three saw him before you planted him?"

John blinked at the crudity of the reference. "As far as I know."

Gilbert sighed. "You're not going to have us dig him up, are you?"

John looked aghast at this suggestion.

Stephen asked, "How long has he been dead?"

John's face pinched as he worked out the numbers. "Let's see. We found him Saturday morning. Today's Wednesday. Five days then?"

Five days, Stephen considered, in this weather, which had been warm for the season. He was tempted, though as repelled as John at the same time. "No, he'll just be full of worms. We'll learn nothing useful."

"Thank heaven," Gilbert said. "The last time we dug up a body, I had to do all the dirty work," he said in partial explanation to John.

John's mouth worked soundlessly at the thought that Stephen and Gilbert had ever done such a thing.

"Where was he found?" Stephen asked John.

"In the cellar."

"And that is — where?"

John waved toward the west range. "Under the lay brother's dormitory."

"Show me the place."

"A moment, sirs, while I fetch the keys."

"Why are you being so hard on the boy?" Gilbert asked as they followed John across the cloister to the long building that formed the western part of the priory.

"I am not being hard on him," Stephen said.

"You were sharp and rude. He seems like a decent boy. There is no reason to treat him so brusquely."

Stephen halted. "Do you not see what the prior is doing?"

"It is obvious that he intends to use us in his battle against Percival FitzAllan," Gilbert said mildly.

"He wants us to accuse him of murder."

"Yes, imagine where that will lead and the trouble it will cause."

"For us especially. What if FitzAllan isn't behind the monk's death? Do you think that matters to our prior? Do you think he will care?"

"I don't know," Gilbert said, troubled.

"He will not be satisfied with any answer that does not implicate FitzAllan."

"You don't think he expects us to lie, do you?"

"I imagine that whatever we learn, which will probably be nothing, that he will twist the facts to suit his purposes. But the word will be out that we are the source of those facts. Don't you think there might come a time when we will be called in to swear about them?"

"I suppose so."

"And consider this — Sir Geoff's first wife was a Fitz Warain, or do you not recall?"

"I do remember that."

"This has to be her manor we are standing on. She must have donated the land to the priory. But who hired the lawyers to defend the bequest in a suit that dragged on many years?"

Gilbert was quiet for a moment. "Sir Geoff, of course. This was her marriage portion of the Fitz Warain lands and came to him when she died."

"Given that, and given Sir Geoff's position and influence at court, do you think that our prior failed to tell Sir Geoff his suspicions and what he hoped to do?"

"I would think not. And if he tarried, Sir Geoff would have them out of him in short order."

"And Hugh wanted Sir Geoff to be here, undoubtedly to give weight and credibility to the investigation. Yet we are here and he is not."

Gilbert looked uncomfortable. "Sir Geoff expects us to do whatever we can to protect the priory."

"You heard him as well as I did. Even to the point of lying under oath."

"Oh dear."

"So Sir Geoff provides the prestige, we provide the lies, and the priory is saved."

Gilbert slid his hands into his sleeves as monks do. "Let us pray that the facts lead to a convenient place after all."

"Yes," Stephen said grimly.

"Sirs!" John called when he saw that Gilbert and Stephen had noticed him again. "Is anything wrong?"

"Nothing you need to know about," Stephen said. "Get on to the cellar."

Chapter 7

The cellar was an undercroft that took up the entire space beneath the lay brothers' dormitory. The gateway passage, rather like a tunnel through the west range, cut the cellar in half so that there was a north and a south cellar, each accessible through a door within the tunnel. Each door was secured by a padlock.

John fumbled with the lock to the north cellar. He pushed the door open and stood back for Stephen and Gilbert.

The cellar was filled with neatly stacked barrels and sacks with aisles between them, stretching into the gloom. It smelled musty, of rye and oats and dirt, and of onions — from the rafters all about hung clusters of onions strung up to keep through the winter. Two cats lying in the dirt, one solid gray and the other a tabby, raised their heads when Stephen entered, and fled down one of the aisles, leaping over a fallen shovel.

"He slept here?" Stephen asked as John entered.

"He slept there," John answered, gesturing to a cubicle to the left. "He was subcellarer, as I said before. Brother Arnald is afflicted with a palsy and has trouble getting around at times. He is often in the hospital, so Brother William volunteered to take his place in the cellar for the last few years."

"It is normally the cellarer's duty to sleep in the cellar," Gilbert added at Stephen's perplexed expression.

"I will need a candle," Stephen said. There were no windows so the only illumination he had at the moment came from what the open door allowed.

"Of course, sir," John said. He went across to the porter's quarters and returned with a pair of lighted candles. He gave one to Stephen and the other Gilbert.

Stephen paused at the doorway to the cubicle. It was perhaps three paces wide and four paces long and contained only a bed with a mattress and pillow, a table and a stool. A couple of pegs driven into the walls for hanging clothing were the only decorations. It was sad, forbidding and austere. It had no window, of course, and must have been cold and dreadful here in the dark of winter.

He bent over to study the dirt of the floor, but as he suspected it had been so churned up by the passage of others that it gave no hint to William's last moments.

"Is that the mattress on which he was found?" Stephen asked.

"Yes," John said. "We've taken nothing out, except for his belongings."

"Those were?"

"Well, we left his other habit. No one wanted that."

Stephen looked at John. "Where is it now?"

John pointed to the wall by the doorway. A sad looking rag hung there from a peg.

"We did take his second pair of shoes," John said.

"I suppose someone else now has the shoes."

John nodded, his face momentarily long. It seemed that he had coveted the shoes.

Stephen knelt, bending close to the gray blanket, almost touching it with his nose. He went over it from the top hem to the foot, turned it over and did the same thing for the underside. Then he turned his attention to the linen sack that was the mattress, which was filled with grass by the feel of it — less prickly than hay, another common stuffing. There was loose dirt on it and dirty smears, as well as a few flecks of brown by the pillow, and a few more such specks on the pillow itself that on casual inspect might have been mistaken for dirt, but were not. He pulled up the mattress, which he probed carefully in case there might be something hidden within the linen sack. There was no reason to think that anything might be, but he had been careless once and he was afraid that he might miss something important.

"Gilbert, John," Stephen said, "would you mind carrying the mattress and pillow into the yard? The light is not good enough even with these candles."

While they were gone, Stephen put Gilbert's candle on the table, and examined the rest of the cell, even going to his hands and knees to inspect the corners and along the bases of the walls. He found nothing but dirt, balls of lint, and rat droppings — except for one oddity. In the dirt beneath the bed there was the clear impression of a hand in the dirt. Stephen held his own over the print. They were similar in size, with Stephen's slightly larger.

On a peg by the door hung a tattered and patched habit. Stephen took it from its peg and went out to the cloister on the excuse to view it in the sunlight, but in truth the cramped room, so filled with the feeling of death and melancholy, depressed him, and he wanted to escape.

Gilbert was bent over the mattress. A few brothers were sitting about the cloister with books in their laps. When Stephen glanced at them, they pretended to go back to their reading, but looked up when his eyes wandered away from them.

"What do you make of it?" Stephen asked Gilbert, holding out the habit to show Gilbert the collar, which was crusted with a dried fluid.

"Looks like blood to me."

Gilbert aligned the pillow with the mattress so that a trickling of brown spots on the mattress matched up with a trickling on the pillow. "See here," he said, pointing to the trickle.

"There's not much of it though."

"Not nearly enough."

Stephen turned to John: "His throat was cut, was it not?"

John gulped and nodded. "Ear to ear. Brother Odo sewed it up for the funeral mass, but you could see it, the stitching, even though his habit was drawn up about his neck."

"Ear to ear, you say," Gilbert said.

"I saw it myself." He added, "Well, Brother Odo did tell me about it. Is that important?"

"Maybe," Stephen said, shifting his gaze to the habit.

"You won't mention that Brother Odo spoke to me about it, will you? The prior instructed him to tell no one."

"Who else might Brother Odo have spoken too?"

"No one, I'm sure! Our beds are side by side and he mentioned it — in passing, you understand."

"I thought you monks were supposed to be silent most of the time."

"Well, yes," John said.

"Are we done here?" Stephen asked Gilbert.

"We've seen all these have to offer," Gilbert said, gesturing at the mattress and pillow.

"I suppose the prior would object if we just left them lying around," Stephen said. "Back to the cell they go."

Gilbert and John carried the mattress, pillow and blanket back into the cellar. Stephen returned the habit to its peg and held the candles for them while they returned the mattress and pillow to the bed.

"Can I tell the servants it's permissible to wash the bed linen now?" John asked.

Gilbert nodded, as he and John left the cell.

Stephen paused at the threshold for a last look about. There were dark spots on the sill. They could merely be imperfections in the wood, but he knelt to see them more closely. Close up, the spot was flaky and dry, clearly not a knot or anything like that.

"Gilbert," Stephen said, holding the candles close to the spots, "come here and see what you make of this."

Gilbert knelt with some effort. He spat on a thumb and scrubbed one of the spots. It disappeared, leaving a small smear on the thumb. "More of the same," he said, as he straightened up from his inspection.

"It would seem so."

"Well," Gilbert said, as Stephen helped him to his feet, "it would make sense. There are no windows in the cellar."

"But the door is locked."

"And the gate is bolted at night."

They stepped into the tunnel under the west range and shut the door.

"The last time they saw him was at the midnight service," Stephen said.

"Matins," Gilbert said. "It's called Matins."

"And by dawn —"

"Prime . . ."

"— he's dead. So whoever killed him got in through a barred gate and a locked door during that interval."

"Assuming that FitzAllan is the killer."

Stephen nodded, glancing past Gilbert to see if John was in earshot, but the young monk had retreated far enough into the cloister that he could not overhear. "And if a monk, merely a locked door, which William might have opened at a knock."

Gilbert shuddered. "I hate to think it could be that."

"Don't we have to consider all possibilities?"

Gilbert clasped his hands, brows knotted with emotion. "We do. I am afraid we do."

"And our William did not die in bed. He was laid there afterward."

"That is obvious," Gilbert said.

Stephen returned to the cellar door. "Here?"

He pushed the door open again and stooped to examine the dirt floor about the doorway. But it revealed no secrets, no sign of a struggle, no evidence of death, even that of a rat, merely the passage of many feet discernible in the dirt. While his hand rested on the door, a thought surfaced in his mind. He said, "He would not have been locked in the cellar at night, would he?"

Gilbert looked thoughtful. "Of course not. I should have thought of that. The cellar would only be locked during the day to keep pilfers out."

Stephen peered around the door. There was a bolt on its interior side. "Quite so. Through a bolted gate and a bolted door then."

He shut the door and threaded the ring of the lock through its iron loop, and the two of them strolled back into the cloister.

"Who was it found him?" Stephen asked.

"Odo. Odo was his name."

"We must speak to this Odo," Stephen said.

A bell sounded in the dormitory across the cloister, and those monks still reading in the open closed their books, rose and went into the dormitory.

"It's time for Nones," Gilbert said. "We shall have to wait."

"More singing?" Stephen asked.

"Show some respect. You're starting to sound like FitzAllan."

Why the mention of FitzAllan's name led Stephen to think immediately of the porter, he could not say. Perhaps it was because it raised the image of FitzAllan and his soldiers arriving for the criminal in sanctuary. Arrival meant visitors and visitors meant porters, although it was doubtful that the elderly porter had gone out to greet FitzAllan.

"The porter —" Stephen said.

"Anselm," Gilbert interjected.

"Don't porters sleep by the gate?"

"Generally, yes."

"I wonder if he heard anything."

"We won't know if we don't ask."

Stephen retraced his footsteps into the tunnel, passing the doors to the cellar to the only other door there, which stood just within on his left, but far enough back that the gate doors could open without covering it. There was a large iron knocker on this door.

"I would say we'll find him lurking there, if anywhere," Gilbert said.

"He has nothing else to do?"

"Not usually."

"They pay a man just to sit around and mind the gate?"

"Normally, it's a brother, older and unable to do hard work. Anyway, how's that any different from a gate warden in a town?"

Stephen rapped with the knocker. A moment passed, then they heard Anselm's voice: "Thanks be to God! I'll be right there!"

The door opened. "Ah," Anselm said. "Our visitors. Do you require something, sirs? May I be of service to you?"

"A moment of your time is all we want," Stephen said.

"I'm an old man, so I haven't many moments left, but I suppose I can spare one or two for you. Come in and have a seat."

There was in fact only a single bench and chair standing by the sole window in his apartment. The shutters had been thrown open and a warming breeze drifted in. Anselm settled into the chair.

"Is your view good from there?" Stephen asked.

Anselm nodded. "It allows me to keep watch of the gate and the yard. But you didn't come to ask about the view. You came about the dead brother. You're to find out that FitzAllan killed him."

"You know about that," Stephen said.

"Oh, certainly. I learn most of what goes on here, eventually. People stop on their ways in and out and often drop a word or two."

"What if it had been one of the brothers?"

Anselm rubbed his thighs. "They've all denied it," he cackled.

"How do you know that?"

"On Saturday, after Simon found William dead, the prior put the question to them in chapter." He added, "You won't mention this, will you?"

Stephen nodded, encouraging Anselm to go on.

Anselm said, "I listened under the windows of the chapter house, see."

When it was apparent that Stephen did not comprehend the significance of this admission, Anselm went on. "I'm not supposed to leave the gate unattended — in case we have a visitor."

"Did you leave the gate when FitzAllan came?"

"I defended my post with courage, though I had naught but a spoon for a weapon."

"And you did not think to hide? I would have, if armed with only a spoon. You saw everything, then?"

"I watched from my window."

Stephen wasn't sure he believed this. He stepped to the window and leaned out to get an idea of the view. He could see all the yard and along the west range to the entrance to the church well enough.

"When did FitzAllan come?"

"Friday morning before dinner. A boy ran up from the village warning that he was on his way. Everyone already knew about Oswic, you see, that he was here and claiming sanctuary. For such an argumentative fellow, he has friends, you know, even here in Lower Clun, and besides, no one on our side of the river has any love for FitzAllan. So I alerted the prior and the brothers were in place at the entrance to the church even before he and his men arrived." He cackled again. "It was a sight! I've never seen a man turn so red in the face. I thought his head would burst!"

"He was angry," Stephen said.

"That's an understatement. I thought he meant to kill a few brothers to have his way with Oswic."

"But he stayed his hand."

"Yes. It was a miracle. The prior said so. The brothers said a mass for their deliverance."

"Did FitzAllan make any threats?"

Anselm frowned. "There was a great deal of cursing, but I really don't recall any threats."

"Do you think it was FitzAllan?" Stephen asked.

"What, behind William's murder? He was mad enough, and he's had it in for the priory for years. If the prior says so, that's good enough for me."

"But you have to admit that it's odd to find William dead in bed."

"The prior says that it was done that way to put the fear in all of us. To send the message that none of the brothers, or anyone who works for them, are safe, even here."

"Did you hear anything?"

"When?"

"On Friday night, after Matins."

"I heard the singing. Usually I sleep through it. But I have trouble sleeping, you know. I often wake up in the middle of the night."

"So you woke up about Matins that night?"

"I did, in fact. I stretched my legs out in the cloister. I even saw Brother William when he came back from the service."

"You did?" Stephen asked, surprised. This meant that Anselm probably was the last person to see William alive, besides his murderer.

"Yes, he said good night, in his usual cheery way, went in and bolted the door. You know, it's really sad that it was Brother William. He was such a likeable fellow. He always had a good word for everyone. And smart as a whip. People said that he might be prior himself one day. No one was surprised when he was appointed subcellarer — that's a very responsible position, you know."

"You went back in your apartment after you said good night to Brother William?"

"I walked a bit more about the cloister. Talked some with Oswic. The singing keeps him up. He likes to complain about it — I don't think that boy is happy unless he's complaining about something. Then I turned in."

Stephen said, "After you went back to bed, did you hear or see anything out of the ordinary?"

"Friday night, you mean? Sometime before dawn, I thought I heard a horse nickering. But I'm not sure. It could have been a dream. I don't know." He added, "The prior says I should say I heard several horses, but I think I only heard the one."

"And that's it? Nothing more?"

"Not a damned thing." Anselm smiled sheepishly and put a finger to his lips at having let a curse slip out. "Not even a yowling cat."

"We will need to talk with each brother," Stephen said. "Privately."

"I do not see why their devotions or work must be disturbed," Prior Hugh said. "I have spoken with them already. None heard or saw anything."

"You questioned the brothers, how? At chapter?" Gilbert asked, although he already knew the answer.

"Yes," Hugh said. "How else was it to be done? It is the best time. They are all together then and it is the purpose of chapter to discuss the business of the house."

Stephen and Gilbert exchanged glances. Brothers may be accustomed to sharing their sins in public but there could be secrets that some might not be eager to disclose.

"Must you?" Hugh fumed. "How long will that take?"

"As long as it takes," Stephen said.

Hugh appeared about to throw out more reasons why it should not be done, but he seemed to have run out of any that sounded reasonable. "Very well," he said shortly. "Tomorrow. I will give over our chapter hour for that purpose. The remainder of our day is too precious to squander on such a wasted effort."

"Have you also questioned the lay brothers?" Stephen asked.

"Why? What benefit is there in that?"

Of course he had not done so, Stephen reflected. Hugh was from a gentry family. Servants were beneath notice in many such households.

"Well," Gilbert said, "they have eyes and ears, just like other men."

"You will take care of that as well?" Hugh asked.

"It will be our pleasure," Gilbert said.

"I doubt that," Hugh said. He pressed ink-stained fingers on the margins of a parchment as if it wanted to leap off his writing table. "Will that be all?"

"Probably not," Stephen said. He rose, recognizing that he had got all he could out of the prior on this subject. He added: "Do you have a scrap of parchment you could spare?"

"What for?" Hugh asked, puzzled.

"I want to send a letter."

Chapter 8

Stephen took the parchment scrap, a borrowed wooden stylus and an ink bottle into the refectory. He sat at a table, dipped the pen, and cleared his mind for the arduous task of putting words down, or tried to anyway. This was not easy to do in any circumstance but was made harder by Gilbert's presence at his side.

"What are you doing?" Stephen asked. "Don't you have a lay brother to harass?"

"This is an opportunity of a lifetime," Gilbert said. "I can't miss a moment of it."

"What is?"

"To see proof of what few of us suspected, that you can put pen to parchment and produce a literary masterpiece, the new Ovid, the new Geoffrey of Wales."

"Who's Ovid?"

"A poet. A much more agile writer than the Bracton you are used to, I imagine."

"Bracton can be hard going," Stephen admitted. Bracton had written a treatise on English law and process that all lawyers had to read. When Stephen had been forced to study the law under crown Justice Ademar de Valence, he had been compelled to immerse himself in Bracton. He would not wish such a fate on anyone. "What did Ovid write about?"

"Erotica, mainly."

"I am surprised your abbot allowed you to read something like that."

"I copied a volume of Ovid once, for a fee," Gilbert said. "The Ars Amatoria, it was called. He didn't know about it."

"I will bet it was the beginning of your downfall. Now go away."

"No, I wish to see your elegant hand so that in future you will not criticize my horsemanship."

"It is not criticism, merely casual observation."

"As mine will be."

"If you have any teeth left."

"Why, that almost sounds like a threat. You better get on with it, whatever you are writing. It will be supper time in an hour and I dare to think it will take you at least that long."

Stephen grunted. He was not, of course, going to strike Gilbert, no matter how much he felt like it. Since the clerk was not going away, he had no choice but to begin.

It took at least half an hour of laborious writing in his best clerk's hand to write out the letter, conscious at every stroke of Gilbert at his shoulder. When he was finished, he produced a small cylinder of sealing wax and a seal from his belt pouch. He heated the end of the cylinder over the fire on the hearth, dropped a dab of hot wax on the fold of the letter, and pressed the seal into the dab.

"There," Stephen said as he blew on the wax to harden it. "Would you return these things to the prior for me?" he asked, gesturing at the writing tools as he started toward the door.

"Where are you going?"

"To deliver my letter."

"But it's to your cousin in Wales! You're not going to desert me here, are you? You promised Sir Geoff you would stay!"

It took a moment for Gilbert to realize he was being had, a span lengthened by his anxiety at being left alone at the priory to investigate the monk's death by himself. Then it penetrated his mind that, of course, Stephen would not ride deep into Wales to deliver his own letter. He scowled, hands on his hips. But before he could say anything, Stephen had slipped out to the cloister and closed the door.

As he strode across the cloister, Stephen gauged the height of the sun, which had dipped so low that it was hardly visible above the roof of the west range. He had only about an hour left until dark. That should be enough time if he hurried.

The bell sounded in the cloister, calling the monks to yet another devotion in the church, for again the habited men in the cloister folded up their books and went inside. Stephen wondered how they got any work done during the day with interruptions every two hours or so, let alone any sleep at night. The lot of a monk was more onerous than he had imagined. Stephen liked few things better than a warm bed on a cold night, and being dragged from it for any purpose after he had settled in was not something he would tolerate even if it happened only occasionally.

He entered the tunnel through the west range. He almost passed by, but he remembered that the porter had taken his sword, as weapons were not allowed within the priory. Stephen felt naked riding about without his sword, especially this close to Wales.

He rapped on a shutter. No "thanks be to God" greeted him this time. The shutters flew open so sharply that he had to step back to avoid being struck in the face.

"Ah, sir," the porter said when he saw who had disturbed him, "your pardon."

"Did I interrupt your nap?" Stephen said.

"I, well, yes. Please don't say anything, will you? I'm not supposed to nap, but sometimes I get so little sleep during the night that I cannot help myself."

"Yes, and it is strenuous work waiting for people to knock so I'm sure you are all worn out."

"Quite, sir," the porter said.

"You have my sword," Stephen said. "I require it back."

The porter disappeared from the window and returned with the sword. "And why would you be needing your weapon, sir, if you don't mind my asking?"

"I feel like a ride in the country, and you never know whom you might run into."

"It's awfully late for that. It will be suppertime soon and you won't want to miss that, not that our fare has been so sumptuous the last few years since the troubles started. And then I am to bar the gate and admit no one. The prior is very strict about that."

"I should be back before dark. And if I'm a bit late?" Stephen prodded his substantial purse, which was swollen with the money Sir Geoff had given him.

"Ah, yes. Very good, sir. Just knock on the shutter, three knocks followed by two, so I'll know it's you and not some nightwalker. Well, enjoy your ride. If I may say, sir, our lands are the safest in England. Lord Percival sees to that, he does. Rules with an iron hand. Step out of line, and he'll hang you quick."

"He enjoys hangings, does he?"

"It seems he does, he has so many of them."

"And not all of robbers, I'll bet."

"No, that's true. But it keeps the grumbling from the villeins down, on his lands at least. " He added, "Some of my kin live under his rule but they only complain of it among the family."

"I'm sure steady hangings ensure the timely payment of the rents, as well."

"They do that, sir. Lord Percival does not like trouble from anyone."

"The poor prior," Stephen muttered. Perhaps the prior was right after all.

"Sir?"

"Nothing."

Stephen crossed the lane to the outbuildings, locating the stables by its low shape and the aroma of horse manure. He went in and noted approvingly that the horses had all been unsaddled, fed and watered. The food at the monks' table might be sparse, but at least they did not shirk proper care of animals, whatever their poverty and troubles. He looked about for a groom, but did not spot anyone who might fill such a role. In the stables of most houses, a groom was always ready on a stool beside the door to serve anyone who came in if he wasn't occupied with some chore. But there was no stool and no groom here. So Stephen laid a saddle pad and saddle on one of the mares, then put on the bridle. The saddle and bridle told the mare that she had to go to work again. She did not want to leave the stall and give up her bucket of oats, and she fought against the bridle and against being led into the yard.

He mounted and trotted down the hill to the village. Where the lane joined the main road, some boys were playing football. They scattered at his approach and regarded him with feral curiosity from behind the wattle fences which separated the cottage yards from the road. One boy skidded a rock in his direction and they all fled behind a cottage.

The mare shied violently at the rock and Stephen nearly fell off. He suppressed a curse and the impulse to chase the boy, who would be long gone beneath some bush by this time. Stephen had shied rocks at riders on the road himself as a boy, so he knew how the game was played, though now that he was the target he had no patience for it and it took a while for the thoughts of vengeance and punishment which bubbled in his mind to subside.

The mare stomped and snored, but horses are easily distracted, and she spotted long tufts of grass growing at the base of an unruly hedge on the left. Stephen let her graze for a moment, throwing cautious glances over his shoulder for more rocks and hoping to spot someone to speak to. But the road was deserted. He gritted his teeth. This was wasting time. He didn't mind riding after dark, but he was not enthusiastic about missing supper if he could avoid that. He was about to head north to the bridge over the Clun, where he was sure he would find a tavern, but then a man in a priest's habit came through a gap in the hedge.

"Good Lord," he gasped, "you surprised me!" He spoke English with a Welsh lilt and the hem of his habit was tucked in his belt, revealing bare legs and feet.

Even English peasants went barefoot during the summer to save shoe leather, but only the Welsh maintained the custom well into the autumn. A pair of young men who looked so alike that they were obviously brothers were right behind him. Like the priest they were barefoot and their black hair was cut short in the Welsh fashion. In the borderlands, it wasn't unusual for English and Welsh to live side by side.

"Your pardon," Stephen said.

The priest noticed the grazing mare and said, "You're feeding your beast on my grass. There is a charge for that."

"Your grass?"

"Well, this is my church, or rather, it's my lord's church. I am its lowly attendant."

Stephen notice now that a small stone church occupied the ground beyond the hedge. He turned his attention back to the priest who was smiling in a friendly way, an indication that his demand for payment for grazing rights had been made in jest. Stephen's first impression was that he was a man at the brink of middle age, but on closer inspection, he seemed older than that, although there was not a streak of gray in his abundant black hair and few wrinkles on the face that were not put there by a propensity for smiling.

While Stephen was considering what to say next, the priest and the two brothers muttered to each other in rapid Welsh — a "get on now" and a "good bye" and "I'll talk to you later" and "watch yourself," if Stephen's very rough Welsh was any guide — and the brothers took off down the road.

"It's late to be out," the priest said to Stephen as he gazed at the brothers' backs.

"I suppose it is."

"Are you the visitor at the priory?"

Stephen was surprised that he knew this. "I am. News travels fast. Or you must have talked to Anselm."

The priest chuckled. "Well, I have known him since I was a boy. The prior has a claim on the produce of my chickens and the milk from my cows, so I must pay a visit every day or two."

"Your church belongs to the manor?"

"All the village south of the Clun belongs to the priory."

"I understand that has been the source of some unhappiness."

"You've met Lord Percival, I've heard."

"You hear a lot."

The priest shrugged.

"How much of what you've heard do you repeat?" Stephen asked.

"Whatever is to my advantage, except for confessions, of course."

Stephen chuckled. "Fair enough." He reached into his purse for a penny, which he tossed to the priest. "I am looking for a horse trader who lives hereabouts."

"That would be Llwyn."

For a moment, Stephen thought he detected a frown of disapproval, but if there had been one, it disappeared beneath another smile. Stephen said, "That's the one."

"He lives that way." The priest pointed vaguely to the west.

"That's very helpful."

"Go down the road about two hundred yards. There is a lane off to the right. Take that. Stay on it about a mile. His house sits on top of a hill above the road. You can't miss it unless you're blind or English."

"As I am English, I shall have to look sharp."

"Are you in the market for a horse?" the priest asked. "I hear you already have three."

"What else are horse traders good for?"

"I can think of a number of things that have nothing to do with horses."

"You are remarkably nosy for a priest."

"The business of strangers is a matter of concern."

"You have your penny. You shall have to be satisfied with that."

"It is a lot for a tuft of grass," the priest said.

"You know it isn't only for the grass. Get yourself a pair of shoes. It will be cold soon."

The priest wriggled his toes in the dirt while he clenched the penny. "No, I think the weather will stay warm for a while longer."

Stephen set the mare to a fast trot. The road curved right and the lane in question was not immediately visible. At the peak of the curve, a lane branched to the left and ahead he saw the one the priest described. He passed the two brothers walking in the middle of the lane. Neither made any effort to get out of the way. Although Stephen could have forced them to give way, he was not interested in provoking them, so he just went around. One shot Stephen a venomous glance, while the other studied the path as if he was not there.

He wondered where the pair were going this late in the day, for the road stretched straight on, bordered on each side by a hedge and open fields, with not a house in sight as far as he could see. Presently, he passed a pair of houses with outlying sheds and a barn and garden lying at the foot of rising ground on the left where a woman was cutting wood in the yard and a boy and girl were playing in the dirt, and Stephen supposed this must be the destination of the surly brothers.

A short distance beyond the cottages, a wood grew about the lane and here the path began a turn to the left. When Stephen emerged from the copse, he saw a broad rolling field on the right where horses, cattle and sheep were grazing, and on the hill still some distance away to the front stood a great wooden tower with the roof of a hall visible beside it.

The hills formed the half of a vast oblong bowl at this place, and at the apex, a switchback ran up the hill to the manor house. A pair of grooms waited just within the gate ready to take his horse and direct him into the hall.

Stephen had hoped to get his business done quickly, but supper was underway already — broth, bread, and apples, from the look of things. The Welsh always ate more simple fare than the English, but Stephen's stomach, so poorly accommodated at dinner, was glad to get this much, since he would be late for supper at the priory and it was doubtful that food could be begged from the cook there after hours as it might be in another house. He was led to a place at one of the side tables and not introduced to the host as he had expected. A servant appeared with the bowl for washing his hands and remained to take the towel when Stephen had finished with it. The hall was filled with the hum of conversation, all of it in that musical cadence of Welsh, that didn't waver at Stephen's appearance, as if it were perfectly normal for a stranger to spring out of the earth and to be seated with everyone else. Down the table, a thick-shouldered man, dressed in a green tunic with yellow stitching that Stephen at first took for gold thread, caught his eye. Given his central position at the head table and the richness of his clothes, this had to be Llwyn. He had a plug for a nose supported by a black beard so dense that it was impossible to spot his mouth even when he opened it. Above the nose a balding forehead rose like a cliff of unblemished alabaster, framed by cascading black Welsh hair. His face exuded confidence in himself and his place in the world. He beckoned to a servant, pulled him close and spoke into the fellow's ear. The servant came over to Stephen and said in English, "My lord bids me to ask your name and your business, sir."

He calls himself a lord, does he? Stephen mused. He said, "I am Stephen Attebrook. Please tell your lordship that a mutual friend sends his regards."

"And who is that, if I may ask, sir?"

"Sir Geoffrey Randall."

The servant withdrew and delivered the message to Llwyn. If the name Geoffrey Randall carried any weight, Llwyn did not give any indication. He did not look at Stephen after that.

A servant bent over and said in Stephen's ear, "Please follow me."

Stephen looked up from his ale cup. After supper, he had tried to speak to Llwyn, but servants had intercepted him and escorted him to a chair, where they had sat him down and put the cup in his lap, firmly and politely, but leaving no doubt that he was to remain there and not to bother the lord. In turn, no one had bothered him, even to talk about the weather or anything else. It was as though he was a leper and might communicate his disease through the merest breath. But now, it seemed he had earned a reprieve.

The servant snared a candle on the way and led him out of the hall and into the wooden tower. They climbed stairs for two stories and the servant put the candle in his hand, left him at an alcove and went away. Stephen wondered what to do now. He heard rustling within the alcove and realized it was a privy and someone was in there.

"So, Attebrook," a voice said from the darkness, "just what does Randall want?"

"He thinks war is coming to the March and wants to engage you to learn Llywelyn's intentions."

Llwyn snorted. "The Prince of Wales does not share his mind with me."

"I doubt Sir Geoff expects you to knock on his door and ask him what he is about. But you know you can learn a lot by talking a stroll among the village taverns and by seeing who is recruiting and whether men have been summoned."

A figure loomed out of the dark and stood over Stephen. Llwyn's breath stank of sour ale. He said, "You don't understand our position."

"Whose position?"

"Folk like me, the Welsh who live under English law. There are those of us who support our English lords, and those who don't, who wouldn't mind having a return to Welsh rule in our fathers' lands."

"Which are you?"

"I'm one of those who just wants to be left alone. War is bad for business."

"Yet you call yourself a lord. The business of lords is war."

"Lord," Llwyn said, "I like the ring of it. Besides, this land owes knight service to FitzAllan, although he takes it in silver instead of iron, and that gives me the right to call myself a lord under English law." He paused, breathing heavily, and Stephen realized that he may be drunk. Llwyn said, "You're coming here, at such a late hour smells of intrigue. There are those who yearn for Llywelyn's coming and keep a watch on their neighbors so that scores can be settled in times of trouble. There are plenty who have scores with me and you've given them an excuse, even if the purpose of your visit is perfectly innocent."

"I've thought of that," Stephen said, fetching his scrap of parchment, which he held out to Llwyn. "I have family in Powys. You can say I came to you asking for delivery of a letter to my son. Everyone knows you do business between the east and the west. No one will think it unusual that I asked you to deliver this."

Llwyn's hand lingered in the air for a moment, then he took the parchment. "They will read the letter," he said.

"It says nothing a father might not say to a young boy, or to his guardian."

"It is expensive delivering letters, especially in these times."

"I have thought of that, too."

"Or someone else has. You don't look like a man who has two pennies to call his own, although that's a fine mare you rode in on, I'll grant you that. Would you like to make her part of the bargain?"

"No."

Llwyn shrugged and named a price in money that was more than what Stephen had in his purse. They dickered over the amount for a few minutes and, at last, Stephen poured silver into Llywn's palm, half the price now, and half when the messenger returned.

Llwyn offered to let Stephen stay the night, but he declined. The sliver of a waxing moon had set over an hour ago, and the night sky was clear and cold, and filled with stars which gave enough illumination to find the way if he didn't look directly at things. The road when he reached it seemed to glow faintly white in the starlight, and the only sounds were the rustling of the wind, the plodding of the mare, and faint voices ahead and out in the field: probably herdsmen who kept watch during the night.

The road wound around the bowl of hills until it reached the shoulder where the woods rose about it, dark and oddly forbidding for such a small woods. Stephen hesitated before entering, listening and considering whether to strike down into the field to ride around it, but he could see no break in the hedge separating the field from the road, and hearing nothing but the wind, he pressed his heels against the mare to send her forward.

Stephen had reached the point where the road curved to the right when a figure darted out of the undergrowth into his path and seized the mare's bridle. Stephen cursed and drew his sword. But before he could pull it fully out of the scabbard, a loop of rope dropped over his head and pinioned his arms. The only thing he could think to do was throw his arms straight out before him, as one would when grabbed over the arms from behind in wrestling. This prevented the rope from closing about his waist, but whoever had hold of the end yanked hard, and the loop caught on Stephen's neck and he fell heavily on his side.

He could barely breath and streaks of light flashed across his field of vision, as he pushed the loop over his head and twisted on the ground to avoid a kick aimed at his body. He had dropped the sword in the fall, but he still had his dagger. He drew the shorter blade, while shielding his head from another kick with his free hand. He struck at the closest target: one of his attacker's legs. But the point only snagged clothing as far as he could tell.

The dagger blow forced the attacker to dance away to avoid the point, which allowed Stephen to rise to his feet. He knew there were two of them, but he had only the one in view and he edged to the side, glancing about for the second man, whom he finally spotted as a vague shape in the dark as the fellow dodged out of the way of the mare, who, free from restraints now, pounded away toward the village.

Stephen realized that the mouth of the copse was behind him and that the two robbers, for that is what they must be, could see him far better than he could see them. The desire to kill them both rose hotly on a tide of anger and humiliation now that he was out of immediate danger. He expected the two to attack, but they hung back, probably wary of the prospect of a knife fight in the dark.

He edged back toward Llwyn's house, dagger out and ready.

He had only gone a few steps when something — a club, he thought — struck him hard on the dagger arm and disarmed him. There was a third man! He rushed blindly at the new attacker, hoping to grapple with him before he had a chance to strike again, but the third man slipped the rush and gained Stephen's back. Stephen tried to spin toward him, but the third man looped a strand of rawhide around his neck from behind and cut off Stephen's wind with a convulsive jerk, pressing a knee to the small of Stephen's back. Stephen struck the knee aside with an elbow and, pivoting, grasped handsful of clothing. Pivoting again, he threw the third man over his leg. Showing he was an experienced wrestler, the third man let go and rolled with the throw, carrying himself completely out of Stephen's grasp. The momentum of the roll allowed the third man to gain his feet.

Then, without a word exchanged between them, the three men crashed through the undergrowth at the side of the road.

Stephen stood panting from the exertion, listening to the diminishing sound of bodies tearing through the wood as the three men clambered up the side of the hill until the night grew quiet again.

Except it was not totally quiet. The air seemed to prickle with an unnatural sharpness — the wind sighing, the branches rattling, the grass rustling, the distant lowing of a cow and the faint clank of metal from the direction of Llwyn's keep. He trembled, as he usually did when a terrible danger had passed. It had been a close thing and he had barely survived, but somehow he had managed it.

Stephen removed the rawhide loop from his neck and rubbed the sore place it had left. The forearm where he had been hit with the club smarted. He would have a good bruise there by morning.

He cast about with his right foot for his dagger, which he found after a few minutes searching, and moments later his sword. "I think I shall register a protest with Percival FitzAllan," he said. "I believe these are his woods."

He had felt depressed and disgusted about the entire affair of the dead monk and having to play spy master. But now, the satisfaction of having survived had driven off the depression. He had come through the fight with only bumps and bruises and wounded pride at having been unhorsed. If he ever told the story, he would skirt over that part.

He set off down the road, sword in hand against the possibility that his attackers might decide to visit again.

A little tune called "The Randy Prioress" popped into his head and he hummed it until he found the mare grazing by the road.

Chapter 9

Despite the lateness of the hour, Gilbert was still interviewing lay brothers when Stephen returned to the priory. Stephen stretched out on the bed in the room set aside for them and tried turning an ear to the interrogations for a while — as it was the only spot were Gilbert could conduct them in relative privacy — but the ones he was privy to were brief and all too similar: I was asleep, I heard nothing untoward, we all liked Brother William, he was such a decent fellow, God rest his soul, poor man, so young and with so much promise. "He was always decent to you," the last one said. "Never lost his temper, even when things went wrong or when you didn't do the work to his satisfaction. And he was quick to laugh."

When Gilbert finished, he sat on his own bed with folded hands, regarding the floor as if the secret might be written there in ink that could be discerned only if he stared hard enough.

"Were they all like that?" Stephen asked.

Gilbert nodded. "Mostly."

"No help then."

"No. Not a bit. What have you been up to? I had begun to wonder if you hadn't struck out for Wales after all."

Stephen told him briefly of his visit to Llwyn's house and the incident on the road, leaving deliberately vague the part about falling off the horse. Gilbert watched him sharply as if he suspected that there was a hole in the story, but he made no comment.

When Stephen had finished, Gilbert took up the candle and said, "Come on now, let's have a look."

"At what?"

"Your neck."

Stephen sat up and Gilbert bent close to look at his neck.

"What's the matter?" Stephen said. "You don't believe me? You think I'm making it up?"

"I rather suspect that you haven't the imagination to make up such a preposterous story. I'm just making sure you aren't hurt."

"I told you I wasn't. And what's preposterous about it?"

"Nasty mark. It will make an interesting point of conversation at breakfast." Gilbert sat back down and returned the candle to the little table that stood between the beds. "Well, you have to admit that it's odd that you would be attacked in a land we have repeatedly been assured was as safe as the inside of a church on Sunday. It's such an out-of-the-way place too — not the sort where robbers are likely to lie in wait after dark, I would think."

"I've thought of that."

"And?"

"Well," Stephen said, stretching out on his bed again, "who do you think is responsible?"

"Sneak attacks in the night are hardly monklike."

"No, they aren't, but clearly we are not dealing with the ordinary monk."

"You don't believe they were monks, though," Gilbert said, but there was a pleading aspect to his voice, as if he did not want to believe the attackers could have been from the priory.

"For all I could tell, one of them might have been the prior himself."

This was not what Gilbert had wanted to hear and his face hardened.

Stephen said, "I certainly don't believe they were FitzAllan's men."

"No?"

"If they had been, they wouldn't have botched it."

"You would know more about the capacity of soldiers for robbery and murder than I," Gilbert murmured. He was quiet for a time. "It could have been FitzAllan men."

"I told you, I don't think that's likely."

"Well, you see, there have been incidents."

"Incidents?"

"Nobody killed, mind you. But many fights and beatings, mainly down in the village, and occasionally in the priory fields, and especially when one of the prior's folk ventures into FitzAllan lands. But now that we've shown up, perhaps the earl has felt goaded to go beyond mere beatings. He knows we've come to pin the blame on him but dares not strike at us openly. Better to do so in the dark when he can blame the attack on others. You're sure you weren't followed?"

"I could have been," Stephen admitted reluctantly. "It was a lonely little road and I didn't bother looking back."

"You shall have to be more careful in future." Gilbert chuckled without humor: "Perhaps it is more devilry from Nigel FitzSimmons."

"I suspect Nigel will not want to incur the expense of tracking me to the edge of England," Stephen said. A couple of months back, Stephen had been in a feud with this Nigel FitzSimmons over the death of FitzSimmons' cousin. They had fought a duel over the matter, and it should have been concluded. But when passions ran hot, endings were not always neat. "If he still bears a grudge, he'll wait until I come into more convenient reach."

"You do have a capacity for collecting enemies: FitzSimmons, Valence. Now FitzAllan."

"I shall consult Harry on how to make friends when we return to Ludlow."

"Ah, Harry. It is so cold at the gate this time of year, and winter's coming on." Gilbert sighed and blew out the candle, plunging the little room into darkness. He said, "I am afraid that we are no closer to the truth than we were yesterday morning."

A bell sounded in the east, faint and seemingly far away. The mournful gong persisted for some time and then fell silent. Stephen turned over to go back to sleep, but Gilbert arose, pulled on his clothes with a good deal of stumbling and clattering about in the dark, and went out. Stephen lay there a few moments longer, before rising.

He found Gilbert on the stairs leading down to the cloister starting at the church, where faint candle light illuminated the unfinished windows. Voices came from the church and the chanting began.

"Matins," Gilbert said, his eyes closed, mouth moving to the words.

It took a moment for Stephen to work out what he meant: the midnight service. He said, "Brings back old memories, does it?"

Gilbert nodded, lips still moving silently to the chant.

"Pleasant ones, I hope, although I cannot see how interrupting a good night's sleep like this can be pleasant. It's too much like standing guard."

Gilbert eyed Stephen. "It is standing guard, on men's souls. Now, hush! I cannot hear the psalm."

"Sorry."

"No, you're not."

"Well," Stephen said, "I am."

The singing continued, and Gilbert sighed. "I wish I could be there." Tears formed in his closed eyes and ran down his round cheeks. His shoulders shook.

A wild impulse seized Stephen of the kind that had often got him in trouble as a boy. He tested the roof of the awning. It was made of planks of wood nailed to cross beams and seemed solid enough to bear a man's weight. He said, "I think there is a way."

"What are you talking about? We can't get out without waking Anselm."

"I wasn't thinking about using the gate." Stephen climbed onto the awning roof. He held out a hand to Gilbert.

"You're mad!"

"Are you coming or not?"

"What if we're caught?" Gilbert looked fearfully across the cloister to the dormitory.

"No one will see. They're all in the church."

Gilbert hesitated. His hand reached for Stephen's but jerked back, his desire at war with his conscience. "I shouldn't do this."

"Of course, not, but you want to."

Gilbert grasped Stephen's hand and climbed up beside him. He said breathlessly, "We could say that it is part of our investigation."

"Yes, I could break into the cellar by climbing on this roof. I am sure our killer thought the same."

"Well, I thought —"

"I'll make up some excuse. Don't worry."

Stephen turned and made his way along the awning toward the church, mindful of the slope. The fall was not far, but he did not relish having to make it. Gilbert followed him just as gingerly.

"I cannot believe I am doing this," Gilbert said.

"Neither can I. It will make a good story when I tell Harry."

"You will not tell Harry!"

"Keep your voice down. They can probably hear you."

Gilbert ducked his head as if he had been swatted, but whispered, "You will not tell Harry, do you hear! Not a word."

"He will enjoy knowing that I've led you into a life of crime. He thinks you are altogether too good."

"You have already led me into a life of crime as far as I wish to go."

"Turn around, then."

But they had arrived at the church wall and it was too late to turn back.

Stephen leaned in the first window he reached. Gilbert stood on tiptoe and looked in beside him. The chanting stopped and the monks began singing in Latin, some sort of hymn. Stephen's Latin, though good enough for reading, didn't allow him to puzzle out the meaning without some effort, which he did not expend. So while he listened to the singing, he examined the interior of the church.

Within the shell of the half-built walls, a series of pillars which were hardly taller than stumps, surrounded by piles of stone and lumber, rose from the grassy floor like the broken trunks of trees and marched down the nave to the altar, which stood under the only part of the church that had a roof. Besides the roof, the altar itself was also shielded from the weather by a shed-like structure built around it. Stephen could see the monks arranged in neat lines before the altar, each holding a candle. Toward the western end, beyond the congregation, there was a small canvas tent erected among the pillars and piles of lumber and stone. A figure emerged from the tent and slipped into shadow away from the singing monks, a figure that was not manlike at all, but womanly. The woman squatted in the lee of a pillar as if doing her business and then crept back to the tent. Her head was visible for a few moments through the flap of the tent, and disappeared inside.

"Well," Gilbert said with disapproval as they climbed onto the stairway, "I hope you satisfied your curiosity."

"My curiosity!"

"I feel as though I've committed a sin," Gilbert said glumly.

"I fail to see how that was sinful. No one was hurt."

"Since when have you cared what God intends?"

"Well, not recently, anyway."

"It would do you good to think more about it."

"You're starting to sound like Edith."

As they entered the west range and closed the door, Stephen asked, "Did you see anything untoward in the church?"

"No. Why? Did you?"

"No."

"Well, then?"

They fumbled down the corridor and arrived at the guest room. As they were disrobing for bed, Stephen said, "You should ask the prior if he will allow you to join the brothers at the dawn service."

"I doubt he will allow it," Gilbert said.

Dawn had not quite arrived when Stephen threw open the shutters to the guest room window. He stuck his head out and looked around. The air was chill and held a distinct snap. Across the way, the outlines of the outbuildings were just discernable. A cock concealed among them crowed and was answered by another, and he heard the lowing of cattle as well.

He was about to pull his head back in when a skirted figure emerged from the church and hurried across the yard to the road.

Stephen nodded, as if the sight held some meaning, but truthfully, it seemed only a point of gossip, which he had not been inclined to share with Gilbert for fear it would be reported to the prior and Oswic's pleasure disturbed. If the law was followed, Oswic eventually would have to go into exile, and Stephen, who already had something of a taste of that experience during the nine years he had spent in Spain, knew it could be bitter indeed to be away from your friends and family in a strange country without any idea when you would get back to familiar ground — and Stephen's exile had been voluntary, fleeing a life he had thought he despised for what he had expected would be wealth and glory. He had found the wealth, but it had been lost, and glory had been his as well, though it had little value now since all those who had witnessed his adventures in Spain were either dead or enslaved. Glory, without other men to speak about it, was only a memory or an arrogant boast. However unpleasant a man Oswic might be, Stephen had no desire to make his life more miserable than it already was and undoubtedly would be again quite soon.

"Is it time to get up?" Gilbert murmured from somewhere deep under his blankets.

"Not yet," Stephen said.

"Ah, no bell?"

"No bell. Why don't you sleep in? You only torture yourself listening to them. It makes you think you made a mistake choosing Edith."

"I wish I could have had both," Gilbert murmured.

Stephen went down to the tunnel through the west range. Anselm's window was shuttered but rippling snores audible through the window boards indicated that the porter was still asleep.

Stephen lifted the bar and pushed the gate open. It screeched like a wounded animal from rust on its iron hinges, and as he slipped through, Anselm threw open his window and called out in alarm: "Who goes there?"

"Go back to bed," Stephen said. "It's only me."

"No one is to enter or leave during the night!" Anselm protested.

"It isn't the night," Stephen said. "It's time to get up."

Anselm squinted in the gloom. "It's still night. Officially. Don't think I'll let you back in until it is true day."

"Full day will be here in half an hour. You'll have no choice."

Anselm continued to grumble, but he closed the window.

Stephen shut the gate and strolled to the west end of the unfinished church.

The wall here was only hip high, and gave the impression not of a building wall but a stone fence for a garden. But instead of a garden the church nave was filled with grass, piled timber and blocks of stone. Some of the blocks were partly squared, and one might think that the mason who had worked on them had just knocked off yesterday, except for the moss that grew on the sides.

As Stephen stepped through the gap meant to be the doorway, he startled a gray cat which had been sitting in the grass with a dead mouse under its forepaws. The cat snatched up the mouse and fled around a large pile of stone that seemed to lean against the wall to the right. A few steps further into the nave, the toe of his good foot struck something; not a stone or a tuft of grass but, vaguely visible in the dawning light, a pile of horse manure, gray and dry and several days old at least.

"He's taken your breakfast," Stephen said to Oswic, who was seated on a pile of stone to the left.

"I've never had the need to develop a taste for mouse," Oswic said. He had a whole onion in his hand and he took a bite from it as if from an apple. "But the way they feed me, I may have to. The priory's hospitality is thin."

"You seem to be doing well enough."

"Oh, I manage. I manage well enough. But it could be better."

"The prior says you are a clever fellow."

"He does not."

"Well, he also says you are disagreeable, and that sometimes leads to trouble."

"I've had my share, that's true. But none if it is my fault, despite what the prior says."

"Do they keep you awake at night?"

"Who? The monks?"

"No, the goblins."

Oswic grinned. "I'm getting used to it. I sleep through it most of the time."

"But not when you first got here."

"I know where you're going with this."

"The prior did say you were clever."

"You want to know what I know about William's death."

"Do you know anything?"

Oswic took another bite from his onion, chewed and swallowed. "The walls are thick."

Stephen glanced at the timber and plaster wall of the west range which was visible above the pile of stone. "They don't look very thick to me."

Oswic shrugged.

"No shouts?" Stephen asked. "No scuffles? No one coming or going in the night?"

Oswic bit his onion again, carefully as if fearful of breaking a tooth. He shook his head, mouth full.

"Did you know William?" Stephen asked.

"Everyone knew William." When Stephen said nothing to fill the silence, Oswic went on, "After the cellarer took sick, what was it now, two years? Three? He became the bailiff for the manor, so he got about quite a lot, unlike most of the others. He also was charged to take the manor produce to Llwyn's for sale since the priory is forbidden the liberty of the Clun market." Oswic was quiet for a moment, peering into the distant sky. He added, "Anselm says you are the coroner at Ludlow."

"Deputy coroner."

"Well, deputy then. But still a royal official and charged with finding William's killer."

"I am."

"Whoever that might be."

"Whoever that might be," Stephen repeated.

Oswic drew a breath and was about to speak when the bell for Prime rang in the east range. He flinched at the sound, and said hurriedly, "They'll be here soon. We can't be seen. Listen, I may be FitzAllan's tenant, but I am a free man and my time is my own to do as I wish and make a living in my own way. I often helped William carry the manor's produce to Llwyn's. I am good with horses and mules," he said with some pride. "He kept two sets of accounts, one for himself and the other for the manor, of what he delivered and how much he was paid."

"Llwyn paid in money?"

Oswic nodded.

"And two sets of accounts, you say."

Oswic snorted. "You really are thick, the way you repeat everything you're told."

Stephen ignored the insult and turned over in his mind the implications of what Oswic had said. "How do you know there were two sets of accounts? You can't read."

"I can so! . . . Well, not a lot, but enough to figure accounts," he said with pride.

Stephen remembered what Hugh had said about Oswic and nodded. "I doubt William would have shown them to you."

"He dropped them once in the road on the way and the wind began to carry them. I picked them up. It flustered him that I had seen them, but he never suspected that I understood what they were."

Stephen nodded thoughtfully. It seemed a facile story, yet it was plausible.

Oswic grinned. "And Llwyn knew. I overheard them talking about it. It was a scheme they cooked up between them. He was cheating the manor every which way."

"Did the prior know?"

"Not until the day before William died."

"How would you know that? It doesn't seem to be general knowledge."

"They argued about it." Oswic pointed to the altar at the far end of the church. "Over there. The prior wanted him to swear an oath on the altar."

"And you've told no one about this until now?"

"If I had said anything, within a day everyone in the valley would know it came from me. Llwyn would've had my head off. He seems a friendly man until you cross him or threaten him. You'll keep my confidence, won't you?"

Stephen nodded. "And the money, the money William kept for himself. What's happened to that?"

"Well, that's the real mystery, isn't it? It was a tidy sum."

Chapter 10

The chapter house was not actually a house but a room on the ground floor of the east range that butted against the south transept of the church.

When Stephen and Gilbert were shown in, there were four chairs set out in the chapter house, three in a line against a wall and one set before them. Prior Hugh occupied the center chair of those in the line and he glanced at Stephen as a monk held the door to admit them. Hugh gestured to the chairs on either side as if giving them permission to take seats. Stephen remained standing. He could feel Gilbert behind him fidgeting with nervousness.

"I will speak to your people alone," Stephen said.

"As you say, they are my people and I will hear what they have to say."

"You've already heard, or so you claim. It's my turn now."

"This is my inquiry."

"No, it's mine, and I'll conduct it as I please, or not at all."

Hugh's thin lips pressed together. "I shall write to Sir Geoffrey. You are being most uncooperative."

"Write whatever you like. I will still speak to your people alone."

They glared at each other for some time. Finally, Hugh rose and stalked from the room. Stephen manhandled one of the chairs away from the line and took one of the pair remaining. Gilbert sank beside him with a sigh.

"You've made him angry," Gilbert said.

"I'm beginning to dislike him. He interferes too much."

"I daresay, he dislikes you."

"Why is it that men with power take disagreement personally?"

"Human nature, I suppose."

"Perhaps he has something to hide that he wants to ensure remains concealed."

Gilbert shot Stephen a hard look. "What do you mean by that? Have you learned something new?"

"I am not sure."

"Oh, dear," Gilbert said, distressed.

Their escort, who had remained at the door and who had witnessed the exchange with Prior Hugh, looked just as distressed.

"Send in the first one," Stephen snapped at him.

The interviews with the monks went no better than those with the lay brothers: I saw nothing, I heard nothing, I know nothing. Even the elderly brother Thomas who had risen frequently during the night had not seen or heard anything strange. "It was an ordinary night," Thomas said, "just like any other."

Young Simon, the last of the novices who had been made a monk only two weeks ago, recalled for them how he had been sent to fetch William when he had not appeared for the Prime service. "We all thought he had overslept again," Simon said with almost a wail.

"Again?" Gilbert asked. "He was in the habit of sleeping late?"

Simon nodded. "He often had to be fetched for Prime. The habit displeased the prior, but since William worked so hard during the day, he made an allowance for him."

"How did you fetch him?" Stephen asked.

"What do you mean?"

"Was the door to the cellar latched?"

"Oh, it always was. I would have to bang on the door."

"Was it the same this time?"

Simon looked puzzled. "No, the door wasn't latched. I thought that odd. Is it important?"

Stephen and Gilbert exchanged looks. "No," Stephen said.

Simon went on, at their urging, to describe the scene in the room when he had discovered William's body, but the boy's powers of observation were such that neither inquisitor could be certain that the room in fact had been left untouched, except for the removal of the corpse.

At last Brother Odo sank into the witness' chair. He folded blunt-fingered hands on his lap. He was about thirty, though deep-set eyes, a flat nose and rounded cheeks. He smiled hesitantly.

"Brother Odo," Stephen said, "we are told you prepared William for burial."

"I did," Brother Odo said. He had a soft way of speaking that was almost a whisper and Stephen and Gilbert had to strain to hear him.

"Did you unclothe him and wash him?" Stephen asked.

"As I always do," Odo said.

Stephen nodded. It was custom. He said, "So you had a chance to examine his body."

Odo looked unhappy, but nodded. "I cannot say I examined him, but I did see."

"What did you see?"

"The prior has ordered me not to speak of it."

"You can speak of it to us."

"I don't know," Odo said.

"Has the prior given you any instructions about what to say to us?" Stephen asked.

Odo shook his head.

Stephen said, "Should I fetch him here? Do you need encouragement to unburden yourself."

"No, sir."

"Then speak. Do not hold back."

Odo licked his lips. "He was marked," he said.

"How so? You mean beyond the wound at his neck?"

Odo nodded. "All over his body, there were bruises, as if he had been beaten. And . . ." he paused.

"And what?"

"There appeared to be burns on his chest and back, as if someone had pressed a burning ember to his flesh. And —"

Odo leaned forward and pointed to Stephen's neck, "— he had marks on his wrists and ankles like the one on your neck."

"Describe the placement of these marks, if you can," Gilbert said, his voice unable to conceal shock and revulsion.

Odo touched himself in a dozen difference places on his chest and stomach.

"And the back?" Stephen said.

"If I may," Odo gestured to Gilbert, who stood and turned around so that Odo could point out the locations of the burns he had observed.

Stephen wished he had made a drawing to record all the spots, but his memory, faulty as it was, would have to do. "About the bruises," he said. "Tell us about those."

"Well," Odo said, "there were none on his face, which I thought was a bit odd, except for some slight wounds in the mouth."

"As if he had been struck there?" Gilbert asked, having now sat down.

Odo nodded. "There was some blood and his lips were cut, but no more badly than you'd expect for a lad in a fist fight. There were some marks on his back, as if someone had taken a stick to him. You'll know what I mean if you've ever seen the results of a caning. But," he shuddered, "the worst of it was on his forearms and shins. There wasn't a patch of unblemished skin anywhere on him." He sighed. "He must have suffered terribly. Who would want to do such a thing to such a pleasant fellow?"

"Do you have any suspicion that William's behavior was . . . less than correct in any respect?" Stephen asked.

"Why, no," Odo said. "Did he do something wrong?"

"I cannot say."

"The poor boy," Odo whispered. His eyes closed and his lips moved slightly as if in silent prayer. He looked up. "Are you done with me now? I cannot bear to think of what I have seen."

"Beaten and tortured," Gilbert said, grimly, "but for what purpose? This was no idle act, no burst of anger. No simple murder." He looked sharply at Stephen. "You know, don't you? Tell me what you've been concealing."

"We have the how," Stephen said carefully, "and perhaps the why. But we are still no closer to the who and where."

"You have not answered my question. You may have the why, but you have not shared it with me."

"You may not like the answer."

"I will hear it nonetheless."

"Very well." Stephen briefly told him of his conversation with Oswic.

Gilbert looked appalled. "You cannot trust that boy."

"Perhaps not, but if it is a lie, it is too easily disproved."

"That may be. The common liar cares only for the moment, and thinks nothing of whether the facts are easily determined."

Stephen smiled without humor. He stood up. "Let us visit the prior. He will know the truth, about that at least."

They climbed the stairs to the second floor where the monks slept. The beds were set with heads against each wall, leaving an aisle down the middle, and Stephen and Gilbert passed down the aisle under the eyes of most of the monks, who had been told to assemble in the dormitory so they could be questioned each in his turn, and had not yet been given leave to disperse. Stephen's back prickled under the force of all those gazes and he could sense anxiety and disquiet permeating the floor like a fog so that he wondered if his suspicions were true and that one of their number knew more than he was telling.

He reached the door at the end of the dormitory and knocked on it.

"Come!" the prior's voice said after a moment.

Stephen pushed the door open and entered.

Prior Hugh looked up from the book he was reading by the window.

"We need a word with you," Stephen said.

"Me?" Hugh said. "You mean to interview me?"

"I do."

"I've already told you everything I know."

Stephen said, "Perhaps not all. Was William stealing from the priory?"

Hugh's mouth fell open. It closed and opened again. He said, "That's absurd. He was as honest as the day is long."

"Not so long this time of year," Gilbert murmured so softly that Hugh gave no indication he had understood.

"He didn't keep two sets of accounts for the shipments he took to Llwyn?" Stephen said. "One for himself, and one for you?"

"I have heard nothing of that!" Hugh said. "Where have you heard this slander? Who said this? I will have the name!"

"So that you can do what?" Stephen said.

"If one of my people has been spreading such a lie, it is a betrayal," Hugh said coldly.

"This priory," Stephen said in a musing voice, "it is an appurtenance of a larger establishment, is it not?"

"What if it is?" Hugh asked, nonplussed at the change of subject and clearly put off that Stephen had refused to answer his question.

"You must report to your superiors for its management."

Hugh waved a hand. "Of course."

"And if you manage it poorly, I assume there will be repercussions."

Hugh stood up. "I think we are finished here."

"I see we are."

"You frightened him," Gilbert said when they were safely down in the cloister and far enough from anyone who might overhear.

"Yes," Stephen said. "I think we did."

"You did. I had nothing to do with it."

"He won't like you any better for it."

"If I continue my association with you, I'll soon have no friends left," Gilbert fretted.

"I didn't know you had many friends," Stephen said. "Innkeepers are notoriously short of them." They reached the passage through the west range and were silent for a while on the chance that Anselm had his ear cocked. In the yard Stephen said, "So who was lying — the prior or Oswic?"

Gilbert sighed. "I did not see Oswic speak so I could not measure him. But I thought our prior was less than truthful."

"I thought so too."

"But you cannot think he had William killed to suppress knowledge of this theft — just to protect his position!"

"Men have killed for less."

"But not one of these men could do such a thing." Gilbert waved behind him at the priory indicating that he meant the monks.

"It doesn't have to be one of them. There are enough hard men on any manor to do the bidding of the lord, even if it includes torture and murder."

Gilbert shuddered. "I refuse to believe it."

Chapter 11

"There is something you can do today," Stephen said, gazing thoughtfully at the entrance to the church. Llwyn's name came to mind, followed swiftly by the memories of a skirted figure in the church and fleeing into the morning fog. He had not wanted to say anything about her, but now, revelation of what he had seen seemed the only course if he wanted to avoid having Gilbert accompany him to the Welshman's house.

"I am always ready to be useful," Gilbert said.

Stephen grinned. "From Edith's complaints, I'm not so sure about that."

"She wants me to do unpleasant things. I am allowed to object to that. What do you want?"

"Last night, and again this morning, I saw a woman in the church," Stephen said. "Oswic's woman, I think."

"Oswic — the boy claiming sanctuary?"

"He said he saw or heard nothing, but he may be less than truthful. Perhaps you can get something out of his woman."

"What is Oswic doing with a woman in the church?"

"What men always do with women."

"Oh dear. Does the prior know?"

"I suspect not, and I also expect you not to tell him," Stephen said more sharply than he had intended.

"But it's sinful to use a church that way."

"It's a small sin that we will overlook, for the moment, since it is to our advantage to do so."

Gilbert shook his head, ready to object.

Stephen said with some exasperation, "It's not the first time a church has been used for a tryst."

"I know, but still —" Gilbert said.

Stephen glared at him and Gilbert glared back. At last Gilbert said, "All right. What is her name?"

"I don't know."

"A fine interrogator you are."

"Ask around the village. Everyone is bound to know who she is. You heard Hugh. She is a tailor's daughter. How many tailors can a town the size of Clun have?"

"Now? Before breakfast?"

"God forbid you should do anything before breakfast."

"A good meal strengthens the mind."

"Too many expand the girth. I'll see you by dinner time." Stephen started back into the west range.

"Where are you going?"

"To see Llwyn."

"But you just saw him yesterday."

"I want to know if he's got anything to say about Sir Geoff's inquiry," Stephen lied. For he had an altogether different set of questions for the Welsh trader.

He turned away.

"Be watchful for robbers," Gilbert said to Stephen's back.

"Three feet of Spanish steel should see them off."

As he passed through the gate, Stephen thought he heard Gilbert add, "Not if they shoot you in the back."

At the village church, Stephen turned the mare right rather than left and rode into what there was of a village on this side of the Clun. Here, houses lined the street down the gentle slope to the wooden bridge and occupied the ground on a lane that branched off the street a short distance above the junction of the road to the priory. And when he reached the foot of the bridge, he noted that the houses went half way to the bend in the road, which followed the river, then stopped where the ground rose abruptly to overlook the road. There were, as far as he could count, two dozen houses on this side, while on the other bank there had to be at least one-hundred-fifty houses, perhaps even two-hundred.

Two taverns sat at the foot of the bridge across the road from each other. Even one tavern would have been unusual for such a small village, but two were a rare extravagance. It had to be due to the traffic that came down the road from

Wales, because they would be the first any traveler from the west met as he arrived. For the road along the river was unusually wide, but he remembered that it was a drover's route and used for cattle and horse drives, and herds could not be confined to a cart track and tended to trample a wide swath through the country side.

The aroma of fresh-baked bread was thick in the air and made Stephen's mouth water. He had come down partly out of curiosity to see the lay of things, partly because the visit to Llwyn promised to be dangerous and he wanted time to think over how to approach it, and partly because, whatever he had said to Gilbert about breakfast, he was hungry, though after the words he had exchanged with Prior Hugh, he was not eager to endure what would surely be a cold atmosphere in the priory's refectory. He did not want to spend the money, but some of the coin Sir Geoff had given him was for expenses, or so he told himself.

Stephen chose the tavern at the very foot of the bridge. It already had its shutters down and seemed more ready for business than the other. He tied the mare to the post at a corner of the building and went up to the window, where he bought four sweet buns smothered in honey. They were so hot he could hardly pick them up and he burned his mouth at the first bite and nearly had to spit out the mouthful.

"Careful there," said the girl at the window.

"Sorry," Stephen mumbled, breathing slowly to cool the morsel so that he could swallow it. At last he got it down and blew on the remainder of the bun. "Not bad."

"Not bad, the man says," the girl said. She was a pretty thing, short and slight and perhaps as much as fifteen, with her hair braided underneath her linen cap, signifying that she was already married.

Stephen liked pretty women as much as anyone, and enjoyed the comfort and pleasure their company provided. He had been too long without a woman of his own and he found himself staring at her, which was impolite. But the girl must be used to strange men staring at her, for she met his gaze with steady, amused green eyes. It occurred to him that if anyone knew the village gossip, this girl did, and that he should question her about Oswic and his woman. But if he did that, it would leave nothing for Gilbert to do, so instead, he looked up the bridge, where two men with swords and spears had come out of a shed on the other side and were looking at him, and not in a friendly way.

"FitzAllan charges a toll to get across the bridge?" Stephen asked the girl.

"A steep one. You thinking about going that way?"

"I had considered it," Stephen said, although he had not. He wouldn't mind poking around upper Clun just to get the look of things or paying a visit to the castle, but clearly he would not meet with a friendly reception if he tried. Besides, he did not have the time. "The tollsmen do not look friendly."

"They're FitzAllan's boys. None of them are friendly, at least not to the likes of us, when they're on duty, anyway." She leaned out the window to get a look at the two soldiers on the bridge, and shouted a curse at them that was so foul, especially coming from the mouth of such a pretty girl, that Stephen was shocked.

One of the soldiers shouted back what he would like to do to her.

"Doesn't that just make them angry?" Stephen asked.

The girl laughed. "The other one's my cousin." She added darkly, "I don't think he'd do me harm. But you never know, if Lord Percival ordered it. But you — they'd like nothing better than to pound your head to jelly, and they could do it too, despite that fancy sword of yours."

"But I am FitzAllan's friend."

"That's not what I heard. You're the prior's man, and Lord Percival hates the prior more than he hates the devil."

"Then I definitely should not cross the river."

The girl laughed. "Not by the bridge, anyway." Someone called to her from within the tavern and she turned away.

As Stephen worked on the third bun, the two young fellows he had seen at the village church yesterday came down the hill and stopped at the tavern.

"Give us a bun, Aelflaed," one of them called. "We're late!"

The other one glanced at Stephen out of the corner of his eye, but otherwise the pair studiously ignored him. Their faces and forearms were scratched, as if they had been in a fight.

The girl appeared with two buns on a wooden tray. "Drinking again into the evening, were you, Brin?"

The one called Brin gingerly lifted his bun and blew on it. "Not me." Although the name, Brin, was Welsh, he spoke English as one born to it, a capacity not unusual for folk who lived in the borderland who could jump from one tongue to another as naturally as changing strides.

"Huh," Aelflaed said.

"We were admiring the stars," the other one said.

"Fat chance of that," Aelflaed said. "Looks like you were in a fight again. Who this time?"

"Nobody you know," Brin said.

Aelflaed chuckled. "Seems he got the better of you."

Both boys snorted. "Nobody gets the better of us," the other boy said.

"I just hope it was on the other side of the river," Aelflaed said. "There's been trouble enough in lower Clun."

The boys shrugged, their mouths full of bun.

"How's your sister?" Aelflaed asked, determined to have conversation. "I haven't seen her in days."

"Caerwen?" Brin said with an off-handedness that seemed to Stephen to be more forced than natural. "She's gone to visit relatives."

"Has she now. She never said anything about that to me. I can't believe she just up and took off without even a goodbye."

"She went to help a cousin who was sick. It came on sudden, like."

"Well, let me know when she gets back."

"I'll be sure to," Brin said. He slapped the other boy on the shoulder. "Come on. Time to go to work."

"You said that already," the other boy said.

"I really mean it this time."

The two of them wandered off to the bridge with another sidelong glance at Stephen. The tollsmen did not bother them other than to exchange words.

Aelflaed leaned on her elbows and watched them go. She sighed and shook her head. "There are a few boys here who are nothing but trouble. That Oswic is one. Those twins are another. Brin and Bran — trouble follows them like a black cloud."

"Why did they not have to pay the toll?" Stephen asked.

Aelflaed said, "They live on FitzAllan land. The plots are all mixed up around here, especially to the west."

"They don't seem like villeins."

"They aren't. Their dad's our priest, Alcwyn. They're free Welsh cotters and prouder than cocks about it. The only thing they can do besides fuss and fight is pound a nail straight and saw a decent board. So they're one of the lucky few who've got work right now because Lord Percival is building himself a fancy stone tower and towers need scaffolds and ladders."

"Towers are expensive," Stephen said, remembering the half-built tower at Stokesay.

"They are. That's why he's squeezing every penny out of all his people. And the harvest was poor again. There's hardly enough left to feed the folk on his side of the river."

Stephen finished his last bun. "It's hard times all over."

"What would you know about hard times?"

"Enough," Stephen sighed. The memory of Taresa knocked on the door of his mind. If he opened it, he would remember her beauty and grace and her terrible last moments as she died of fever, her breaths coming slower and slower until, at last, they had simply stopped, while there was nothing he could do but hold her and rage at God and fate for taking her away. He refused to open that door and finished his last bun.

Aelflaed looked him up and down as if assessing the threadbare state of his clothes for the first time. "At least you have enough to eat."

"I have that," he said, "but little else."

Stephen finished the last bun and regarded the soldiers on the bridge. "Will you do me a favor?" he asked Aelflaed.

"That depends on the favor."

"In a short while a little fat man will come by here. Tell him I said not to cross the bridge after all. It is not safe."

The taste of the buns, rich with yeast and honey, lingered in Stephen's mouth as he mounted and rode up the hill toward the village church, its slate roof just visible above the low growing wall of hazel that surrounded the churchyard. His mind fixed on the problem of how to handle Llwyn, he nearly missed the sight of the fresh grave in the yard, but a splash of brown spied through a gap in the hazel caught his eye. Stephen halted the mare and stared at the mound of fresh earth. On top of it, someone had left a handful of flowers. That seemed an odd gesture from the friends that William was likely to have.

Stephen brought the mare around to the churchyard gate. It was meant only for people, not horses, and was so narrow that the mare barely fit though, and he had to crouch over her neck to avoid the overhanging hazel branches.

It was the only fresh grave in the yard. There was no marker, but few of the other graves here had them. They were marked instead by dips in the tall grass.

He slipped off the mare. The missing toes on his bad foot began to itch as they did sometimes when they did not actively ache. He sat on the grass, removed his boot and massaged the stump. Aside from soaking it in hot, salty water, this was the only way to make the itching stop, which could be maddening if he did nothing about it.

While he sat there, a few people, mostly women, trickled out of the church. They crossed the yard, throwing glances in his direction but otherwise pretending not see him, although he had no doubt that this sighting would be the subject of village gossip and that before dinnertime everyone would know that he had visited the grave and sat as if on a picnic before it: he could hear the talk now — what a strange rude man, so disrespectful of the departed. And the priory expects to find the murderer with the likes of him? Cluck, cluck, cluck.

Stephen sighed, less at the prospect of being the subject of unflattering gossip than the fact he had no confidence that he could find William's murderer, given how little he knew and was likely to know. Although the people in Ludlow seemed to have come around to the idea that he had a knack for finding out things, he had the good sense to realize that his success was the result of dumb luck and not craft. If he had the knack for anything, it was overlooking the painfully obvious. He wished he had a better way to make a living. Standing castle guard could be mind-numbingly boring, but it was a much easier way to make a shilling. You couldn't get rich as a castle guard, but the work was steady and he could probably do it, even with a bum foot. Nobody had to know about that. The thought even crossed his mind that he might eventually rise to castle constable. You didn't have to be able to fight to manage a castle, and he considered that he knew enough about that job not to make a mess of it. When he was done with this miserable business, he would look into a change of situations.

Perhaps, he thought, he should just do as Hugh wanted, declare that FitzAllan was the most likely culprit, and get it over with, and be off to fetch Christopher before the March burst apart with war.

He wondered with Gilbert would think about that.

It was quiet for a time after the last parishioners had departed. The itching in his foot subsided. Stephen held the foot to keep it warm in the chill and contemplated the fresh earth and the bundle of flowers so withered already he could not identify them. He had never paid much attention to flowers and did not know the names for most of them, any more than in the past he had paid particular attention to graves. Graves were everywhere, like flowers and old tree stumps, and normally nobody paid them much mind or considered what lay within them unless it was the remains of a relative or someone you knew. And until recently, Stephen would not have spared a thought for this or any other grave, but now that he was in the business of death, of determining how and why people died, he had begun to see such sights not as objects in the landscape but as individuals who had a tale to tell, if only you listened hard enough. It was disturbing and he hated it. He wished he could go back to being the way he had been: comfortable in his indifference.

Alcwyn, the priest, appeared at the church door. He spotted Stephen, hesitated and came across the grass to him.

"What are you doing?" Alcwyn asked.

"That's William under there, isn't it?"

"What makes you think so?"

"As far as I know, the priory has no graveyard of its own. It takes a consecrated church to have hallowed ground where people can be safely buried, and this is the only one I'm aware of that's convenient."

Alcwyn smiled thinly. "It's amazing that FitzAllan hasn't thought of that."

"Clearly you have not thought to tell him. Otherwise, that Oswic fellow would have dangled at the end of a rope long ago."

"So you're paying your respects?"

"Such respects as I have to give."

"People generally kneel. They don't sit."

"As you can see, I have an injury. I beg an indulgence."

"It's on your foot, not your knees."

"Are you as unbending with your parishioners?"

"No, I don't really care."

"Who left the flowers?"

"I have no idea."

"Not you."

"Of course, not me."

"Some woman perhaps?"

"I cannot imagine why a woman would leave flowers on the grave of a monk."

"Perhaps she loved him," Stephen said, thinking of Edith Wistwode and Gilbert. He had no idea how they had come to be together, but their love for each other was stronger than he had ever seen in any couple.

"It is forbidden. It must have been one of his friends at the priory. He had so many."

"Yes, he had no lack of friends. A personable fellow, from all I've been told. Did you know him?"

"We spoke. When he came to collect the rents."

"I get the impression that you did not like him."

"I . . ." Alcwyn paused. "I liked him well enough. He came here for business, not for friendship."

"Business does not preclude friendship."

"He came, he took, and he went. He did not seem inclined to want my friendship."

"But you must have had something in common. You are both men of God."

"He was English, and the worst kind, a Norman. Like all of that sort he looked down on those who were not."

"It has always been my impression that everyone looks down on those who are not like them."

Alcwyn chuckled. "That seems to be true, doesn't it?"

"So you looked down on each other and shared no confidences."

"I am a humble person, for my part. But no, we shared no confidences."

Stephen laced up his boot and climbed to his feet. He said, "Well, this has been pleasant, but I must get back to work. You can't solve murders by sitting in the grass."

Chapter 12

The day had dawned cool and cloudy, but by the time Stephen reached the turn off to Llwyn's house, the clouds had scattered to wisps and the sun beat down so brightly that he had to squint to take in the pleasant view of the valley with its forested slopes, the river and the town in the distance. It would be warm today, which was always welcome, for the prospect of winter and huddling about the fire brought no joy to anyone. Warm winter days were as precious as gold or a good meal.

Others besides Stephen were enjoying the warmth. He glimpsed a fox in the high grass, an unusual thing to see in daylight. A hawk stooped on prey further up the hill, and a few paces up the road two pheasants strutted into Stephen's path, then flew into the field to the left at the sight of him.

At the gate to Llwyn's house, he paused to wait for a train of at least twenty laden pack horses to file through, escorted by ten men armed with spears, longbows, axes and one or two swords. A pack train was so common a sight that no one but boys paid much attention to them, and Stephen barely glanced at it as the horses filed out.

A series of objects tied to the last horses caught his eye: small kegs made of new yellow wood. A few he could see had a dandelion mark burned on them.

It felt as though he had been struck by a sudden cold gust of wind. Goosebumps popped out along his spine, and he shivered, disbelieving what he saw, alarmed and frightened at what it meant.

Stephen cantered after the pack train, which had taken a narrow path southward toward the summit of the hill. The men at the rear of the train looked at him with suspicion as he closed up.

"Those kegs," Stephen said, "where did they come from?"

His question provoked sneers and the guards did not seem inclined to answer. One said, "They belong to the lord."

"Llwyn?" Stephen asked.

"No, FitzAllan."

"They carry salt, don't they."

"How would I know?"

"Because you know exactly what's in each sack and barrel. Everything's been accounted for and written down. In fact, I'm sure that you have a copy of the list. I know how business is done."

The leader did not reply. He sat on his horse, stone-faced.

Stephen reined close to one of the packhorses. The keg on its back had a bung on the side. He drew his dagger, speared the bung and twisted it out of the hole before any of the escort could more than shout.

Salt spilled out. Stephen returned the bung before more than a handful had been lost.

"You'll have to pay for that," the leader said.

"What's a handful of salt worth?" Stephen asked.

"A shilling," the leader said.

"I doubt that." Stephen dug in his purse and produced a penny which his tossed at the guard who had spoken to him. "Where are you taking them?"

"To my mother's house," the leader said. "No, to market. They pay dear for salt in Wales."

"I'll bet they do," Stephen said, turning his horse back toward the gate. He murmured, "I'll bet they pay dear for lots of things there."

Stephen rode into the yard and crossed to the hall stairway, where Llwyn waited.

"Come to see off your letter?" Llwyn smiled. He seemed the picture of good humor, a broad smile parting his black beard.

At another time, the good humor would have put Stephen at ease, but now it made him wary. For all Llwyn's affability, Stephen sensed an underlying ruthlessness, and he did not need Oswic's caution about it. Stephen's position had become doubly dangerous. What he had come to learn was enough to provoke Llwyn, and now there was what he strongly suspected — no, what he was convinced about. For while the proof was thin, it was obvious to Stephen that FitzAllan was behind the robberies on the Shropshire road and that Llwyn, by selling the fruits of the crimes, was his confederate, and thus equally guilty. Stephen forced himself to relax. He said, "You mean you didn't send it yesterday evening?"

"I am not that eager to do Sir Geoff's bidding." Llwyn nodded toward the gate. "It's just left this morning. They'll be back in a few days with your news."

"Let us hope that Llywelyn does not stir."

"What brings you here this morning?"

Stephen did not want to throw out his question without preparing the ground for it. He wasn't sure how to work up to it and had been hoping for some inspiration. He had no inspiration, so he had to find a way of putting off his reason for the visit. Movement in the paddock on the other side of the yard caught Stephen's eye. A stallion was trotting about within it, agitated by the men who stood about at the railing. Stephen said, "That is a fine horse."

"He is fine," Llwyn said, "but trouble. I have a mind to break him today. He threw one of the boys yesterday. Broke his arm."

"That is unfortunate. What is he worth to you?"

"A horse like that? Twenty pounds at least."

Twenty pounds — you could almost buy an entire knight's fee for that amount of money. "He's not worth that yet."

Llwyn grinned ruefully. "True. He has to be ridden first."

"And trained." A broken horse was not yet fit for battle. He had to be accustomed to the clamor, to the sight of swords and lances swinging into his field of vision, which spooked most horses; he had to know all the small cues that the rider gave with his legs alone to manage him without the reins.

“I’m told you have a stallion of your own,” Llwyn said. “Did you train him yourself?”

Stephen nodded. “I took him in a raid in Grenada. One of my mares is his mother. I raised him from a colt.”

Llwyn led the way to a paddock. The stallion, who had approached a pile of hay by the gate, perked up at their approach and backed to the center of the paddock, watching them cautiously.

“He does not like people,” Stephen said.

“Not at all. And he’s a biter, to boot.”

Llwyn lifted a halter from a post by the gate. “Perhaps you would know what to do with him.”

“I could ride him by nightfall.”

“A handsome boast,” Llwyn said.

“It’s not a boast.”

“I shall have to see this.”

The desire to finish his business and be away to a safer place warred with the prospect of working with the stallion. Horses brought odd, particular pleasure. The allure of a great horse was something Stephen could never describe in words, and would never even attempt to do. No man ever could, not even poets. Words were inadequate vessels for conveying the awe of the stallion’s beauty, his grace, his supple power, and the sublime feeling when you were finally able to bend that power and beauty to your will. Stephen wondered if pleasure could be made to serve business. He said, “If I can sit on him without falling off by, you’ll owe me a whole pheasant.”

“I don’t have a pheasant.”

“You’ve some on your fields. I flushed two on the way up. Send a boy to catch one. You can eat it if I fail.”

“You mean I should pay your wager with my own game?”

“I thought this was FitzAllan land. That means the pheasant belongs to him, doesn’t it?”

Llwyn grinned. “Well, that’s so.”

“So you lose nothing. And if your boy knows his business, perhaps he will catch two.”

"There is the fine, if I am caught," Llwyn said with a sly smile.

"Well, then, I will be good for it, if his warden finds us out. I would not mind dining at FitzAllan's expense."

Llwyn contemplated this proposal for a moment. He spoke to one of the workmen by the paddock fence. The workman singled out looked disappointed at being deprived of the anticipated spectacle, but turned away without obvious complaint.

"If he catches one, there won't be time to cure it," Llwyn said.

"I don't turn my nose up at gamey pheasant, particularly a FitzAllan pheasant."

Stephen unbuckled his sword belt, accepted a halter from one of the workmen, and slipped through the gate. The stallion's ears drew back and it promptly whirled and trotted to the far end. When Stephen followed, he trotted along the rail keeping as far from him as he could.

"You haven't taught him to come when called," Stephen said, with mounting pleasure. He liked working with horses. Each had its own personality that you had to puzzle it out, but none was as troublesome as a person for eventually you could get your way with a horse while with people that was often difficult.

"We haven't taught him anything, not even to quit kicking when we get close," Llwyn said.

Clearly, the stallion knew that the halter and the man together foretold something unpleasant and he would do his utmost to avoid allowing Stephen to get near him. At one point, the stallion kicked at Stephen with his hind legs, provoking an outburst of laughter as Stephen jumped back out of the way.

"Fetch me a bucket of oats," Stephen said.

"That's cheating," Llwyn said.

"Our wager only mentioned sitting. It said nothing about the use of oats."

Llwyn knew very well what Stephen had in mind, for this was a trick as old as tamed horses, and while he could have refused, he signaled to another workman to fetch the bucket.

When the bucket arrived, the stallion regarded it with perked up ears. When Stephen rattled the contents of the bucket, the stallion took a step toward him, but came no closer. But when Stephen approached, still swirling the bucket, the stallion did not trot away, and when Stephen put the bucket under his nose, the stallion thrust his head into it with such force in his eagerness to be at the oats that he nearly drove it from Stephen's grasp.

The stallion's preoccupation with the oats allowed Stephen to loop the halter rope around the stallion's neck. Stephen waited until the stallion had finished the oats, then put on the halter. The stallion, as he had been warned, tried to bite him before he had the halter fully over the animal's ears, but Stephen merely tapped the stallion on the nose with a finger and pushed his head away. The stallion shook his head at the halter, obviously not happy with its presence.

A lengthy switch leaned against the fence by the gate, and Stephen now took it up. The stallion gazed at the switch, white showing about his eyes. He's been whipped before, Stephen thought.

Stephen moved to the center of the pen and let the halter rope play out to the end. He brought the point of the switch near the stallion's flank. The animal shied from it and pulled so hard that Stephen almost lost his grip on the rope. Instead of striking the stallion, however, he gave him the merest touch.

It was enough to get the stallion trotting, and Stephen pivoted so that the stallion trotted in a circle around him. Whenever the stallion felt inclined to drop into a walk, a slight touch of the switch was enough to keep him trotting. Now and then, Stephen applied the switch to inspire a canter, but he did not force the horse to maintain that gait for long. Just long enough, and frequently enough so that the stallion became accustomed to taking commands.

They worked for at least two hours. A call from the house for dinner came and he ignored it. So did Llwyn and the workmen, who stood around the fence to watch, and the servants of the house finally brought out dinner to them and they ate where they stood. The second hour gave way to the third and the sun reached its zenith and began to slide toward the western horizon. So as not to tire the horse, Stephen alternated the trots with walks, and occasionally he let the horse stand as he approached and caressed its head, speaking softly of his admiration of its strength and beauty. He moved around it, touching it everywhere, careful when he moved behind the stallion for kicks, which did not come now. Now and then, he rewarded the stallion with water and oats, and a quarter of an apple which someone had left on his wooden trencher.

"I'll have a saddle, pad and brushes," Stephen said to the assembled audience. "And a sack of grain. The biggest one you have."

"He can't eat a sack of grain," Llwyn said.

"He's not going to eat it," Stephen said.

Stephen brushed the horse down and put on the pad. The stallion was not used to having anything on his back and he shied again and his ears fell back, indicating his displeasure. Stephen had another apple fetched and fed a quarter to the stallion. While he ate, Stephen lowered the saddle onto the horse's back. This was an even greater inconvenience than the pad, but this time, the horse displayed his unhappiness with a shiver of his shoulders. Carefully, Stephen cinched the girth.

Then he took the horse back through trotting and cantering in a circle.

When the stallion had about half an hour of this, Stephen had one of the workmen bring in the sack of grain. The two of them tied it to the saddle. The stallion did not like this extra weight at all, and, when it was secure, he pranced and bucked in an effort to relieve himself of this unwanted burden. But it was tied too well for him to shake it off, and after a few minutes, he gave up.

Stephen resumed the circle exercise, going no more quickly than a trot this time.

This went on for another hour. The horse was tired now from all his work, so Stephen let him walk more than trot. When he judged the time was right, Stephen had the sack removed, and fed the horse another bit of apple.

Most of the day had passed by now, and the sun was no more than a couple of hours above the horizon and the air had begun to chill. The tower cast a long shadow over the pen and the men clustered about it.

Stephen let the stallion stand and he rubbed his neck, speaking softly and encouragingly of his admiration for the horse's hard work.

As he reached the horse's right, Stephen grasped a handful of mane, and boosted himself so that he lay across the saddle on his stomach. He expected to be thrown off, but the stallion stood still. Stephen eased himself to the ground, careful of his bad foot, which had ached for some time from all the standing. He boosted himself up to the saddle several more times, testing the horse. At last, instead of lying cross-wise on his stomach, he swung his leg over the cantle. But he did not linger, slipping almost immediately off the left side. He had to remount now, this time from the left, and because he had no toes for the stirrup, it was harder to do. He had to put his bad foot so far into the stirrup that, if the horse made trouble, there was a danger that the foot would go completely through the stirrup, trapping his foot. People often died when that happened. But the horse accepted the weight without obvious complaint. Again, Stephen did not linger in the saddle, but immediately swung off to the right. He went through this exercise at least a dozen times, carefully watching the horse and sensing for the gathering of tension that would herald bucking, even though that would come, if it did, with lightning swiftness. But still the stallion suffered Stephen's weight.

At last, the moment came when Stephen did not immediately dismount. He stayed in the saddle, grasping the mane with one hand and the halter rope with the other, holding his breath, his entire concentration in his seat for the slightest protest from the stallion.

The stallion did not object. He turned his head once to look at Stephen and, as if resigned to the fact that the man would not go away, the horse turned his head forward, his ears upright rather than plastered rearward.

Stephen slipped off the stallion for the last time and fed the animal a handful of grain out of the palm of his hand.

"Have you caught my pheasant?" Stephen asked Llwyn.

"We have," Llwyn said. "I have never seen a horse broken like that. Where did you learn how to do it?"

"In Spain. A friend taught me. He was a hard man, and often cruel, but he had a soft spot for horses and hated to abuse them."

"I shall have to remember how it is done."

"It isn't hard. It just takes patience."

"Like pursuing a woman."

"Something like that, I suppose," Stephen said. "Although I doubt a woman would appreciate the comparison."

Llwyn's men had caught three pheasants, so supper was an elaborate affair. There was even a bean soup which actually contained chunks of bacon that Stephen found delicious enough that he stood and toasted the cook, who occupied a space at a lower table and accepted the attention with pleased surprise. It was clear the cook was not used to receiving praise of this order.

After supper, with dusk fading into night, with the fire heaped up and throwing its welcome warmth throughout the hall, with the drinking bowls full, with a man and three women singing in Welsh to the company of a flute that trickled notes like the melody of a mountain stream, Stephen sat with Llwyn by the hearth, still not having discussed the matters that had brought him here. It was pleasant to sit here with the ale seeping to his toes, and it seemed a shame to bring up matters that could cause trouble.

"What will you do when the war comes?" Stephen asked.

Llwyn considered the question for some time before answering. "Gather my stock, go into the hills and wait until things quiet down. But you did not come here to talk about war."

"No, I came to talk about Brother William."

Llwyn was quiet for a time. "What do you want to know?"

"Who killed him, of course."

"I cannot help you with that."

"Perhaps not directly. You knew him, though."

"Slightly."

"You did business."

"Through him for the priory."

"But it was more than that."

"It was never more than that."

"You knew he was stealing from the priory, that he received more from you in money for the goods he brought for sale than he returned."

"Let's just say that I suspected it. Not at first, mind. But later. He kept two purses, you see. One for himself and one for the priory. I saw that much and suspected the rest."

"One thing strikes me as curious," Stephen said. "FitzAllan has the priory under embargo. No one is supposed to buy and sell from it, or have any traffic with it whatsoever. Yet you do so, at great danger to yourself, I'm sure. How do you make it worth your while?" Stephen paused to give Llwyn a chance to respond, but when the big man said nothing, he answered the question himself. "You keep an inordinate amount of the price of the priory's goods for yourself, of course." Yet that did not seem a full explanation. He had a further inspiration. "FitzAllan knew about your arrangement with the priory and you split the proceeds with him so he enriched himself from the monks' labors."

Llwyn glared, but said nothing.

Stephen went on, "William found out as well, of course. He knew what was sold and the cost of things. So it wasn't hard for him to work out. And you paid him for his silence."

Their eyes locked. Llwyn said, "What do you intend to do about this?"

"Nothing," Stephen said, hoping to conceal the disgust he felt. He knew he should tell Prior Hugh, but there were reasons he could not. Although he could call it duty, it felt like a betrayal. "Sir Geoff likes your letters. Though perhaps you have additional light you can shed on William's death."

"I've told you all I know."

Stephen sipped again from his bowl. "Why would William steal from the priory? By all accounts he was an upstanding fellow."

"That I do know — it was the oldest reason. He had a woman." A servant paused to refill Llwyn's ale bowl. Llwyn waited until he had finished, then continued, "He was not a man for sharing confidences, but he spoke of her to me occasionally. At supper, much like this one now, and he drank a little too much strong ale. You know the effect too much ale can have: a man who feels sorry for himself cannot conceal it."

"I do not believe that just because he had a woman he felt compelled to steal."

"He planned to leave the priory for her. He thought he might gain employment as a manor bailiff, but that takes time, you know. And until then, he needed something to live on."

"She is a local girl?"

"Indeed, she is."

"You know her."

Llwyn spat into the rushes covering the dirt floor. "Caerwen, Alcwyn's daughter."

As the singers slipped into another song, it seemed to Stephen as if their voices came from far away and a great hush had fallen on the hall.

"I'm told," Stephen said after some time, "that she has left the village."

Llwyn cocked an eyebrow. "You are better informed than you let on."

"It is said that she left to help a sick relative."

Llwyn chuckled. "And if you believe that, I have a spavined horse I'd like to sell you."

"That's not the reason?"

"That's the one her father gave out."

"It's not true?"

"He paid me to have her taken to Llanllwchairn. Alcwyn has no family there. She's staying with one of my cousins."

Stephen did not know the place and racked his brain to remember if he had ever heard of it before. Then it came to him: it was a Welsh village about twenty miles from Clun. "What is the reason?"

"Caerwen is pregnant."

"That hardly seems reason to send her off. Girls are always getting with child without benefit of marriage."

"Prior Hugh can be strict. He is unhappy that Alcwyn had a wife and children. He may not take it well that one of his monks has a child by Alcwyn's daughter. Alcwyn fears for his position. He serves at Hugh's sufferance and that may be the straw that breaks Hugh's patience. Have you got what you wanted?"

"Not yet. Who else knew that William was stealing from the priory?"

"No one, as far as I know. He was very careful. Such a clever fellow. I could have used a boy like him."

Stephen thought about what it all meant. Beyond the fire, he spotted a face that seemed familiar. The man stared back at him. It was one of the guards from the pack train that had departed this morning with the stolen barrels of salt.

Chapter 13

Stephen rode slowly down the hill to the road, listening to all the sounds around him — the wind clattering in the trees and its hush on the grass, the call of a distant voice, the murmur of music from the hall punctuated by talk on the palisade at Llwyn's stockade, the thump of the mare's feet on the lane. They were ordinary sounds, but this evening, with the cockeyed smile of a waxing moon poised above the western hills, each one seemed magnified and menacing, filled with the possibility of danger.

He paused at the road to listen more intently. He drew his sword, the memory of the assault the other evening fresh in his mind. The sword might not protect him from a surprise attack, but its weight in his hand made him feel better.

Stephen studied the way back to Clun. The road along the hillside stood out from the black and gray of the hill as an intermittent light-colored slash, looping around the U bend before disappearing into that copse across the way. It was fairly open here. Trees grew randomly, and waist high hedges along the road and tall grass offered the only concealment, while above but too far away to be threatening, woods covered the upper slopes of the hills. But that copse was another matter. If Llwyn had been behind the attack in the little wood, it seemed unreasonable that he might try the same thing again. But Stephen was unwilling to take the risk. He had been lucky the last time.

Rather than attempt the copse, he left the road and cut up the hill toward the crest, which was shrouded in forest. Even leafless with a spray of brilliant stars overhead, it was so dark among the pine and oak that he could not see his way. A low branch struck him on the face and nearly knocked him off the mare. He dismounted and led her through the trees.

Well into the wood, Stephen heard the sound of muffled movement and he froze. The noise continued to the right and then there came the racket of something dashing through the undergrowth. He turned toward it, sword ready to meet whatever threat approached, but the sound diminished, going off into another direction.

A fox probably, he said to himself.

After what seemed like several miles but could only have been a few hundred yards, he felt the ground descending and abruptly reached the end of the forest. A broad field sloped down to the road, where the square forms of several houses clustered by it.

This time of night the houses should have been dark, for country folk rarely stayed awake past sunset, except occasionally to gather around the fire for story-telling and enjoy the last conversations of the day. But one of the huddles was lighted and not just from the hearth. As Stephen drew closer, a light moved from one window to another: a candle being carried.

Stephen approached the houses, thinking that it would be easier to get through the hedge bordering the field here. He reached a wattle fence enclosing a back garden and as he made for the corner of the fence, the back door to the lighted house slapped open and several men emerged. Stephen stopped behind a spreading juniper and waited. If they saw him, the men would accuse him of trespass and he would have no defense to that, since he had no legal reason for being in this field, nor lurking behind the house.

There must have been a latrine pit at the rear, because Stephen heard the sound of men pissing in long streams as if they had been drinking too much ale.

One of the men spoke in Welsh so rapidly that Stephen, whose Welsh was poor, could only make out a word here and there. The Welshman asked a question and, to Stephen's surprise, he heard Alcwyn's voice answer, joined immediately by the voices of the twins, Brin and Bran; at least he assumed it was the both of them for he recognized Brin's from the morning and assumed the other was his brother.

When the unidentified Welshman had his answer, he spoke again so rapidly that Stephen could not get the sense of what he was saying. He thought he caught the word castle in the rush, but he wasn't sure. He made out, ". . . what length? What length must the ladders be? That's what I need to know."

Brin said, "Twenty-one English feet, I tell you."

"You're sure?" the Welshman said.

"We've suitable ladders," Brin said. "They are the proper height."

"Good," the Welshman said.

The men withdrew toward the house. Stephen peeked around the leaves of the juniper in time to see the door close behind them. He wondered why the twins would be doing business about ladders this late at night. But he had no answer and dismissed the question as he strained to look and listen for any sign he had been detected.

He waited a few minutes to be sure that all was calm before he led the mare around the fence to the road.

Stephen put the mare into a vacant stall and left her oats and water. He crossed the lane from the stables to the priory close. He rapped on Anselm's window, and presently the porter threw open the shutter.

"Oh," Anselm said, "it's you. You'll be wanting in, I suppose."

"I would appreciate it," Stephen said. "I hope I didn't wake you."

"A dead man couldn't sleep through all the racket we've had tonight. Everyone's been wondering where you got to, with all the trouble."

"What trouble?"

Anselm pulled the shutters closed, and after a few moments, the gate screeched open. "I'll have to get that fixed," Anselm said. "It's loud enough to wake the whole village."

"A little oil should do it, I think" Stephen said as he stepped through into the entryway.

"Oil, you say."

"Oil. What's this about trouble?"

"Up in the hospital," Anselm said. "You'll see, oh yes, you'll see."

The hospital was nothing more than another room in the west range down the corridor from the guest room.

Stephen fumbled his way in the dark down the corridor and entered. It was, as Anselm had hinted, surprisingly busy for a Thursday night. A girl of about four lay in a bed to the right. Prior Hugh sat on one side, feeding her broth from a bowl, while a woman who had to be the girl's mother from her anxious expression, sat on the other. The girl coughed, then sneezed. The mother wiped her nose with a rag.

"Open up," Hugh said, proffering a spoon.

The girl opened her mouth as requested and accepted the spoon. It was hard to tell whether she liked the broth.

In the next bed was a pregnant woman in labor. A midwife wiped her forehead. Brother John, who sat on the other side, had a hand on the woman's bulging belly. "It's coming soon, father," John said.

"Thank you, John," Hugh said. "I'll finish here shortly."

Hugh glanced at Stephen and said in response to Stephen's perplexed expression, since it was unusual to find a woman in child birth in a priory hospital, "She's already delivered three here. They all lived so she believes we bring good luck."

"I hope you do," Stephen said. Childbirth was always a dangerous time for women. Most babies came out all right, but often there was trouble and either the baby or the mother died, sometimes both.

In the bed beyond the pregnant woman, lay a boy of perhaps ten. Even the candlelight could not disguise the ashen color of his face. An arm in a splint lay at his side. The boy said, "Can I have some more soup, father?"

"You've had your share," Hugh said. "Try to get some sleep."

"I can't sleep."

"Try anyway."

"It's too noisy."

Hugh smiled. "It is that, but keep trying."

Stephen was about to turn away, but the figure on the furthest bed raised a hand.

It was Gilbert.

His face was swathed in bandages.

Brother John and the midwife helped the pregnant woman to her feet and out the door to another room so she could deliver in private. The little girl finished the last of the broth, and the prior went out. The girl's mother slipped into bed beside her.

The boy said, "Can you put out that candle?"

"No," Stephen said. "Not yet." He fetched the prior's stool and sat down by Gilbert. "What happened to you?"

"I had a mishap."

"I can see that. It looks like you've been kicked by a horse."

"It's not as bad as that."

Now that he was closer, Stephen saw that Gilbert had bruises about his chin and cheek, and he feared it was worse under the bandage. "Let me see," he said. He reached for the bandage. Gilbert flinched and closed his eyes. There was a nasty cut under Gilbert's right eye shaped like a crescent moon.

"I can't wait until Edith sees this," Stephen said with dismay. "She will be furious that I didn't take better care of you."

"It took four of them," Gilbert smiled.

Stephen was glad to see that he hadn't lost any teeth.

"Four of whom?"

Stephen expected Gilbert to say robbers, or something of the sort. But Gilbert said instead, "FitzAllan men."

"The name of Oswic's woman is Leola," Gilbert said with some pride at this discovery.

"What about the FitzAllan men?"

"She comes from a good family."

"I think the prior said something about that already. I'm waiting."

"They have a small house at the top of the hill. It's next to her father's."

"Get on with it. FitzAllan, what about FitzAllan?"

Gilbert sighed. "That pretty girl in the tavern told me not to go across the river. I should have listened to her, I suppose. I know the earl dislikes the prior, but I never suspected that his ill humor would extend to me. I didn't think he even noticed me when we met him."

"You are harmless," Stephen admitted. "What happened?"

"Well, of course, I went to speak with her."

"Of course."

"Which meant that I had to cross the bridge."

"Naturally, since you cannot fly."

"There were some unpleasant men on the bridge."

"The toll takers."

"Yes. They let me pass unmolested."

"That surprises me. Then what?"

"Well, I stopped to ask for directions, and four soldiers came up. It was as if they had just sprung out the ground. Amazing really. They asked me my business and who I was, and when I gave them my name and told them what they wanted to know, the biggest one knocked me down. He was very rude."

"I'll say."

"I got up right away, however."

"You did?"

"Yes, right after I grabbed that big fellow's leg and made him fall down. I even managed to strike one of them, but I'm afraid to say they handled me very roughly, as you can see."

"Good for you." Stephen smiled thinly.

"That they handled me roughly? Thank you very much."

"No, not about that. Four to one would have handled anyone roughly."

"Even you, I expect."

"Even me. You don't happen to know their names, would you?"

"I am afraid I didn't ask for introductions. Should I have?"

"No, but I would like to know who was responsible, that's all."

"Why? What are you going to do?" Gilbert said with some alarm. He started to sit up. Stephen pressed him back.

"Nothing," Stephen said. "I don't suppose there's anything we can do."

Chapter 14

Stephen's fury had subsided to a cold anger by the time he awoke on Friday morning to the ringing of the bell for Prime.

Wrapped in a blanket, he cracked the shutter to admit some light, and contemplated the pitcher and bowl on the table between the beds with some dread. It was chilly and the prospect of washing was not appealing. Nevertheless, he tossed aside the blanket and washed his face and upper body, shivering at the cold.

He threw on clothes and went to the hospital room.

The little girl and her mother were still asleep. The pregnant woman was no longer pregnant, but had a child swaddled beside her. She was awake and their eyes met, and Stephen said, "A boy or a girl?"

"A boy," the woman said. "That makes four boys. I wonder what I shall do?"

"They say girls are more trouble than boys. You just turn the boys out in the morning and hope they come back for dinner in one piece," Stephen said.

"That's what my husband says. But they eat so much. They're hungry all the time. I wonder how we will feed them all."

The next bed was unoccupied. The lad there had already gone home.

Gilbert was snoring in the last bed. Stephen looked down on him for a few moments, and went down to the refectory.

Stephen wondered what to do while the fraterers's servants brought bread and cheese for breakfast and the monks filed in from their service. The prudent course was to do nothing. But the more he told himself that, the more upset he became. He had never been good at turning the other cheek. He felt as if he had been personally insulted, as if he, not Gilbert, had taken the beating.

He could have used a conversation to divert his thoughts, but monks were not allowed to talk at meals, so he made no attempt to engage anyone and no one spoke to him. Even

Prior Hugh, who probably could have ignored the rule of silence, acted as if he was not there, evidently still holding a grudge from yesterday.

Stephen pushed away his empty trencher, washed his hands in the bowl of water provided for that purpose, and got up from the table. Not one of the monks looked in his direction when he went out.

He stopped at the foot of the stairs up to the lay dormitory, hand on the railing. He should go up there now. He should not go through the gate. There were thoughts he needed to think, evidence he needed to remember and evaluate, plans that needed to be made, people who needed to be questioned and questions that still needed to be asked even if there was no possibility of receiving suitable answers. The solution to the murder may be beyond him, but he at least needed to go through the motions before he declared FitzAllan responsible so that he could get about the more important business of fetching Christopher before fire and sword swept the March.

But he did not take the stairs.

Anselm was at his window by the gate, gazing out into the world beyond the cloister. "Going out?" Anselm asked.

Over Anselm's shoulder, Stephen spotted a stout walking stick leaning against a chair. It was quite long, coming to the height of a man's chest, and it had a round knob on the end. Stephen said, "May I borrow your stick?"

Anselm glanced back at the stick. "What for?"

"I feel like going for a walk."

Anselm eyed Stephen suspiciously. "That's hard to believe."

"I have a bad foot. I need the assistance of a stick."

Anselm looked down. "Your feet seem fine to me."

"Do you want to see it? It's quite disgusting."

"Some other time." Anselm hesitated a moment, then passed the stick through the window.

"Thank you," Stephen said.

He went through the gate.

"I want it back in one piece!" Anselm called to his back.

Stephen waved without turning around. When he reached the road, he turned toward Clun.

The pretty girl at the tavern by the bridge, Aelflaed, came to the window with a smile that evaporated when she saw Stephen's face.

"Those two at the bridge," Stephen said, looking at two soldiers sitting on the bridge railing, "were they in on it?"

Aelflaed wiped her hands on her apron, leaned out the window and ducked back. "No."

"Do you know who they were, the ones who beat my friend?"

She did not seem to want to answer, but at his glare, she said, "Tostig, Edward, Martin and Brachwel."

"Where would I find them?"

"Probably at the castle, though one or two of them might be at the Deer, even if it's a bit early."

"The Deer?"

"It's a tavern on the other side. Go through the river gate and follow the road to the right. You can't miss it. You're not going over there are you?"

"On the bridge, is one of those men your cousin?"

"No."

"Thanks," Stephen said. He hefted his walking stick to one shoulder and started toward the bridge.

"You're not going to kill anyone, are you?" Aelflaed asked.

"An eye for an eye," Stephen said over his shoulder. "Isn't that what the book says?"

"I warned him!" Aelflaed called at his back. "I told him not to cross over! You're making a mistake!"

"Probably," Stephen replied, but only he could hear.

As his feet hit the wooden planks of the bridge, the doubts and the anger evaporated. All that remained was cold purpose and iron concentration. He seemed to be walking on air, as if he glided over the ground rather than stepping on it. Stephen had felt this state many times and gave himself up to it, for it was welcome, even pleasurable. A man fought his best when his mind was empty like this, like a pool in the moonlight. Doubt and fear brought injury, death and defeat.

The two soldiers hopped down from the railing and faced Stephen as he approached, long spears in one hand and the other on the pommels of their swords. They knew who he was.

The soldier to the right, opened his mouth to speak as Stephen came within distance, where he could touch them by taking only a single step. Stephen did not give the man the time to say anything. He delivered a mighty two-handed blow at the soldier on the left, aiming the knob at the man's left ear.

The soldier reacted instinctively as he had no doubt been trained to do for such a surprise. He had held the spear upright with its butt on the ground, and it was simple matter to lean the spear to the other side of his body, placing it in the path of Stephen's blow.

Later, Stephen might embellish the story by saying that he had intended what came next, but the truth was, he had not even considered for an instant either how he would attack or what he would do if his initial blow failed. Yet as soon as the stick perceived the lean of the spear, it jerked as if on its own accord around to the soldier's right side and came down with all Stephen's strength on the point where the neck joins the shoulder.

The soldier collapsed in a boneless huddle.

Without pause, Stephen swung toward the other man. But instead of standing to receive the blow and parry, he stepped back out of the way, and Stephen's stick swiped the air.

The soldier stepped back twice more and brought down the spear so that now Stephen faced a prepared enemy who stood behind a glittering iron point at the end eight feet of ash.

A spear can seem an awkward weapon, ungainly and slow, but in the hands of a man who knows how to use it, a spear is as fast and as deadly as a dragon's tongue. This man knew his business. He kept his lead hand steady for aim and with the other at the butt slid the pole forward so that the point danced with a series of quick thrusts which Stephen avoided only by slipping back himself.

Stephen had hoped to overwhelm them both before they had a chance to react, but now he was stalemated.

The soldier made no attempt to finish him, but instead called, "Out! Out!"

It was the hue and cry, the call given to summon the neighborhood to apprehend a criminal.

It was probably best now that Stephen retreat, having done the damage he could rather than face the mob that would show up in moments.

The soldier looked behind him to see if anyone was coming to his aid.

Stephen saw his opportunity. He dropped the stick from the wrath guard, where it had waited above his shoulder. He grasped it with one hand on the butt, and the other midway down its length, and he stepped forward with a shout.

The soldier glanced back, saw Stephen was coming and thrust out the spear one more time, no doubt expecting that Stephen would impale himself upon the point.

But Stephen was ready for this. He swept the spear aside with the tip of the stick. He grasped the spear pole with his left hand, dropped his stick and closed to wrestling distance. Before the soldier could respond any further, he swept the man's lead foot and the soldier fell to the planks. Stephen jerked the spear from his hands and smashed the butt on his jaw. The man's helmet came off and rolled away. Stephen struck him a few more times for good measure, careful, however, not to hit him on the dome of the skull, for his intent was to injure, not to kill.

The street on both sides of the bridge was filling with people who had come out at the call to see what was happening. Stephen watched them, the spear in his hands. He hoped that no one would come near and no one did. The people on the lower Clun side stared gap-mouthed at the spectacle. Someone cheered and in an instant, everyone on the south side of the river was cheering. The people on the north side stared quietly.

Stephen said to the crowd, "My name is Stephen Attebrook. Yesterday, a crime was committed against my friend. If your lord wishes to pursue this matter further, have him send his best man here tomorrow at noon and we will conclude our dispute with sword and shield."

Silence filled the air, solemn and heavy.

Stephen kicked the loose helmet into the river and tossed the spear after it.

He retrieved Anselm's stick and walked back the priory.

Chapter 15

The battle fever had drained away by the time Stephen returned to the priory, and doubts returned about whether he had done the right thing. The possibility of a fight with sharp steel was never something anyone in his right mind looked forward too, no matter how a man bragged about his fighting prowess. The truth was, a fight with sharps often turned as much on luck as skill, and so was an extremely dangerous enterprise. Stephen's stomach quivered at the thought that tomorrow he would probably have to face another man in a fight to the death. But the challenge had been issued, and unless cool heads found some way to avoid it while preserving the pride and honor of all involved, he would have to fight.

As impossible as it seemed, the news of the business at the bridge had already reached the priory ahead of him. When he passed Anselm's staff through the window by the gate, the port gave him a big grin and said, "Glad to see you in one piece, sir. It's about time, sir."

"About time for what?" Stephen said.

"Oh, I'm sure you know," Anselm said, and at the sight of some of the workmen across the road, he leaned out the window, waved the staff, and roused a cheer.

Stephen went through the passage to the cloister, intending to take the stairs to the hospital room and tell Gilbert what had happened. But Gilbert was in the cloister, a bandage still around half his face, with the prior. Gilbert looked anxious. The prior looked angry.

"Come," Hugh said and turned on his heel.

Stephen did not like being ordered about as if he was a mere boy, nor did he think that the prior had any business being angry at him, since the affair at the bridge had nothing to do with the priory. But Gilbert, clasping his hands, followed the prior into the east range. Stephen hesitated, feeling obstinate, and went after them.

They climbed the stairs to the prior's chambers. The prior sat behind his table. Gilbert remained standing. Stephen took a seat on the prior's cushioned chair without being invited to do so. He crossed his legs and folded his hands and waited. The prior said nothing.

Hugh put his face in his hands for a moment, then looked up. "What are we to do?" he asked.

"You?" Stephen said. "Nothing. It is not your affair."

"You are my guest. Your acts reflect on the priory."

"The matter will be settled one way or another by tomorrow."

"Stephen," Gilbert murmured. "You did not have to do this on my account."

"It was not on your account," Stephen snapped. "The insult was as much to me as to you — more so, since I have the means of striking back while you do not."

"It wasn't necessary."

"Of course, it was necessary. FitzAllan is a bully. The only way to deal with a bully is to hit back at him. Turning the other cheek only encourages men like him."

"But he has a castle and so many men!" Gilbert said.

"If FitzAllan has even a shred of honor, it will be settled man to man."

"He has no honor," Hugh spat. "Even if you win tomorrow, he will find a way to finish you."

"How many are there in the garrison?" Stephen asked.

Hugh knitted his fingers and creased his brow in thought. "Fifteen perhaps, and the constable, who is a knight. Not to mention the bailiffs. He has six of them and they are more trouble than the soldiers, for they get about more. This business of broken heads, it's quite common, I'm afraid to say. None of our people dare to cross the river, and the bailiffs assault those of us who are even on our own lands in the west."

"Bailiffs don't count," Stephen said. "Fifteen and a knight. I'd say the odds are about even."

"Even?" Hugh said. "Don't be silly."

Stephen said, "Gilbert will tell you I'm worth at least a dozen archers."

"I wouldn't go that far," Gilbert said, sensing that Stephen was not being serious, a point that Hugh had missed. "Maybe an archer and a half."

"Hush!" Stephen said. "You have such little faith."

"What if he goes to law over this instead of taking up your challenge?" Hugh asked.

"If he does, we counter appeal for the harm to Gilbert," Stephen said. "If he has the sense of a decent leader who wants to keep his men's loyalty, he won't expose his own to the risk of a judgment. Besides, broken heads are common in the March and nobody takes that business to the sheriff. The law is weak here and the sheriff cares very little for the troubles on the March if they don't involve the Welsh. Men settle their own affairs face to face. You know that. So a man who cannot or will not stand up for his rights has none."

"I'm afraid that's so," Hugh said. "It should not be that way."

"But that's the way it is, and no amount of hand-wringing will change it."

"So you will fight tomorrow," Hugh said.

"On my own behalf, not the priory's. I tried to make that clear at the bridge," Stephen said.

"I shall have our carpenter make you a coffin," Hugh said. "Just in case."

"I met Edith," Gilbert mused, unprompted and for no seeming purpose, "on a market day. I was a subcellarer, like William, and that day I was given the task of superintending our servants and bringing our harvest of pomegranates to market." He sighed. "Baskets of pomegranates."

They were sitting on one of the cloister's benches. The sun was warm on their faces and the air balmy, too pleasant a day for mid-November. Dinner was still some hours away, and Stephen's stomach was already rumbling with hunger. The mention of pomegranates did not help.

Gilbert said, "I sold her a basket of pomegranates. She smiled at me. We spoke. I cannot remember now what we talked about. Odd that." He looked at the sky. "It was as if I had been struck by lightning. I can't remember much about that day but the baskets of pomegranates, her eyes and her smile." He rubbed his thighs. "We cellarers are the only members of the community who get out much, you know. We are supposed to be armored against temptation, but my armor was not thick enough, I'm afraid."

"No one faults you," Stephen said.

Gilbert looked sharply at him with his one uncovered eye. "I fault myself."

"You should forgive yourself."

"Mostly I have."

"But not completely."

"When you fail at something so important, you can't help feeling bad about it. I imagine that poor William had such a moment with his Caerwen as I did with my Edith — the moment of shock and irresistible attraction that overwhelms the best intentions — and the regret that follows, but it is not enough to stop you."

"But a chance meeting does not make a romance."

"No, it doesn't. Nor did it make mine. We had no opportunity to meet alone, you see, for I was always under the eyes of my superiors or my brethren. We saw each other perhaps once a month at market and exchanged a few words. Not enough to arouse suspicions, I'm sure. It was the letters that did me in, eventually."

"Letters?"

"Yes. We had so little time to talk on those market days, so we exchanged letters. I stole little waste scraps of parchment or velum and scribbled things on them to her. She's unusual in that, you know. She can read — and write. For she wrote me back." He sighed heavily. "She writes beautiful letters. After a year, I knew I could not remain in the house with thoughts of her in my heart. So I crept out one night and walked to Ludlow and knocked on her door. God be praised that she took me in. I am a failure as a monk but I have tried not to be a failure as a husband."

Gilbert rubbed his thighs again. "There is one thing I am sure of. William would not have had the chance to woo his Caerwen or get her with child during the day. He would always have been under observation by someone who would disapprove. It must have happened at night."

"After the midnight service."

"Yes."

"That gate makes a terrible racket and Anselm sleeps poorly. There is no way he could have gotten out without someone knowing."

"So it would seem."

They sat silently in the sun while Stephen considered the problem. There were no windows in the cellar for William to slip through, and he undoubtedly knew about the danger that noisy gate presented. He could have got out one of the upper windows, but that meant he needed a way down, a rope most likely. He would have to leave that dangling and the window open, which created additional risks of detection.

Suddenly, he remembered a gray cat and an onion. It was not possible, it was so unlikely, he thought. Yet his breath came short in his throat, from excitement or whether if he was afraid his guess would be wrong, Stephen was not sure.

He stood up.

"What is it?" Gilbert asked.

"I have had a thought," Stephen said.

"Oh, dear God. Should I take shelter?"

Stephen stepped swiftly across the cloister. "No, you should hurry."

"It is a crime, if not a sin to make a man of my age and in my battered condition hurry anywhere," Gilbert said, panting for breath when the two of them reached the entrance to the church. He put his hands on his knees and struggled for air, wheezing, "What are we doing here?"

Stephen did not answer. He strode into the church. Oswic was lying on a pile of building stone that rested in a patch of sunlight. Oswic sat up and removed the stem of grass from his mouth.

Stephen said, "Oswic, do you remember when we talked last?"

"Why should I remember that?" Oswic said.

"You were eating an onion."

Oswic looked annoyed. "I was?"

"Yes, you were."

"So what?"

"Where did you get it?"

Oswic's eyes shot away, as if he had just glimpsed something in a corner. He said, "The monks left it for me, of course. As part of my dinner."

"Monks don't give away whole onions for people to chew on."

"Yes, they did."

"You got it from the cellar."

"That's impossible."

"There is a way in."

"Don't be silly."

"You know where it is."

"Nonsense. Did one of FitzAllan's boys knock you on the head or something? You sound mad."

The tabby cat peaked at Stephen from behind a pile of stone to the right. The cat ducked out of sight, and reappeared as it made a dash toward the gap that should be the church door.

Of course, Stephen thought.

He went around the pile. The wall of the church rose to about chest height here, but at ground level, almost obscured by tall grass and weeds, there was a hole in the wall. It was tall enough and wide enough for a man to fit through on his hands and knees.

A sound like the rushing of a great wind filled Stephen's ears as he knelt and crept into the hole.

The tunnel was not long, a bit longer perhaps than the height of a man stretched out full length that ran through the stone of the church and a wall of wattle and plaster. At the end of it, Stephen's forehead brushed a wool blanket hanging across the portal. He held the blanket aside and glimpsed barrels and sacks only a few feet away that seemed to be arranged to form a barrier about the mouth of the tunnel. He slipped through and stood up. He was in the cellar. Somewhere in the dark, he heard the mewling of kittens.

Gilbert was waiting in the nave when Stephen emerged from the hole. He had caught his breath, but otherwise appeared anxious and perplexed.

Stephen stood up and brushed the dirt from his clothing, recalling the filthy habit that had been hanging from a peg in William's chamber. The tunnel explained why it was so dirty. William had worn his worst habit on the passage through the tunnel so as not to leave traces on his best one, the one the brethren saw during the day. A filthy habit did not seem inclined to be the thing to impress a pretty girl, but maybe she didn't notice in the dark.

"Where's Oswic?" Stephen asked, looking around for the young Englishman.

"He ran off," Gilbert said. "As soon as you went into the hole. It really leads into the cellar?"

Stephen nodded. "He really ran off?"

"Like a hare with a hound at his heels."

"Which way?"

Gilbert pointed vaguely to the west. He said, "It seems we've found our murderer, although we've let him get away."

That had been Stephen's immediate conclusion too. He was about to agree, when he remembered his promise to himself not to leap to conclusions, even ones that seemed obvious. "Perhaps so, but perhaps not. Perhaps he was not alone."

"Why do you say that?"

Stephen pointed to the pile of horse manure just within the church doorway. "Do horses generally graze in churches?"

Chapter 16

"It's old," Gilbert said, kneeling beside the pile. "It could have been put down any time before William's death, weeks ago, most likely."

Stephen drew his dagger and cut open the pile. It was greenish within its dry brown shell. "It's not been here more than a week," he said. "Tonight is one week since William's murder."

Gilbert straightened up. "I am sure you are more familiar with the qualities of horse manure than I."

"I shoveled enough of it as a boy," Stephen said, "not so far from the Broken Shield, too." Before he had been sent to London to study law under the renowned crown justice, Ademar de Valence, he had spent several happy years as a squire to the Genevilles in Ludlow castle. Squires were made to do groom's work as punishment for infractions, and Stephen had collected quite a few for a tendency to speak his mind when he should be silent and for engaging in behaviors that were not thought fit for future knights, such as scaling the tower walls as if they were cliffs.

"He could have told us who they were," Gilbert said.

"And you let him get away."

"You should have warned me what you were about to do. I could have taken precautions."

"You couldn't have stopped him anyway." It was, Stephen reflected, his fault and not Gilbert's. He had been more intent on finding the hole than in considering what Oswic might do when he found it.

"The hole and Oswic's involvement rule out anyone at the priory," Gilbert said with undisguised satisfaction.

"I suppose so." Stephen cleaned his dagger in the dirt, returned it to its scabbard and stood up. "It doesn't rule out FitzAllan. In fact, Oswic has a lot to gain, if FitzAllan is involved. A promise of freedom can buy a great deal of silence."

"Why would Oswic linger here, though?"

"FitzAllan lets some time pass so that no one can connect him and Oswic with the death. Then Oswic disappears. People would say that he just ran off, but in truth he turns up on the manor of one of FitzAllan's dependants miles from here."

"A clever scheme."

"It sounds good, doesn't it?"

"If you're right, Oswic will have gone to the castle."

"A sound guess."

"Perhaps it wasn't so clumsy of me to have let him go after all. Admit it."

"What? That you had it planned?"

Gilbert grinned. "Of course."

"All right," Stephen said, "I will credit you with that accomplishment. We don't have the time to argue over it."

He spun about and strode rapidly out of the nave.

"What are you doing now?" Gilbert called, struggling to catch up.

"If we ever hope to speak to his woman," Stephen called over his shoulder, "we must hurry. What was her name?"

"Leola!" Gilbert said, waddling as fast as he could go and with a noticeable limp that Stephen paid no heed to. "But why the haste! You're not thinking of going across the river now! It's suicide."

"We must get to her before she learns that Oswic has fled. If she's willing to spend nights with him here, she will go to him immediately, and we'll never have a chance to talk to her."

Stephen descended the stairs to the cloister. While he waited for Gilbert, Prior Hugh emerged from the chapter house, saw him and came over, curiosity written on his face about what Stephen was up to now. He reached Stephen just as Gilbert emerged from the kitchen with a pair of cloth satchels.

Gilbert said, "He has lost his mind."

"Has FitzAllan agreed to fight you now?" Hugh asked, perplexed and astonished.

"He means to cross the river and question Oswic's woman," Gilbert said.

"Why?"

"Oswic has fled," Gilbert said. "We've found how the killers got into the cellar."

"What?" Hugh said, even more astonished.

"There is a hole in the wall of the church that leads into the cellar," Stephen said. "William had been using it to get out at night after Matins to meet his lover. Oswic must have seen him and told the killers about it. Undoubtedly he saw them put William's body back. If he knows, his woman knows. She spent the nights in the church with him and has to have seen what he saw."

"Lover?" Hugh sputtered. "William had a lover?"

"Alcwyn's daughter," Stephen said. "They were very busy on their nights together. He got her with child. That's why he was stealing from the priory. He was planning to leave and marry her, and he needed a nest egg to get started on his new career."

"Good God!" Hugh exclaimed. He looked as though he might faint with shock. But he recovered and said more calmly, "Why not wait till nightfall? If you're seen, FitzAllan will kill you for trespass."

"If we wait," Stephen said, grimly repeating what he had told Gilbert, "she won't be there. I have to go now."

"This is not sensible," Hugh said.

"If FitzAllan kills me, you have more against him than the mere murder of your monk," Stephen said. He took the satchel from Gilbert's hands. It held a half loaf of bread, freshly baked by the aroma, and a lump of hard cheese: not exactly a feast, but it would have to do. "Try to keep the tongues from waging around here," Stephen said. "I can't seem to fart without everyone in the village knowing about it. Now, tell me quickly about the town."

A hundred yards or so before the lane reached the ford across the Clun, a farm track branched off to the east. Stephen took the track at an easy trot, the satchel on his saddle pommel. He let the reins rest on the mare's neck as he ate, trusting the horse to keep to the track. The day was growing warmer as the sun rose, and Stephen had begun to sweat with the heat.

Still, he enjoyed the ride for the moment, as he tried not to think about the risk.

He glanced back to see how Gilbert was doing. The little man was bouncing along with one hand on the saddle pommel and the other in his satchel and did not seem to be enjoying either his ride or his meal.

Presently, the track petered out into a field dotted with hay ricks that had not yet been gathered in. Sheep and a few cows wandered among the ricks, grazing on the stubble left after the harvest. Stephen startled the herdsman, who was only a boy, taking a leak against one of the ricks. The boy stared opened mouthed at the sight of them, for it must be unusual to see people on horseback on this lane.

So much for secrecy, Stephen thought. But perhaps they could outfly the gossips. At least the trees along the Clun shielded them from view by anyone on the FitzAllan side.

He finished the bread and cheese and put away the satchel. He asked the mare for a faster trot and then a canter as they neared a hedge. He should have turned aside and taken the gap in the hedge to the right. He hadn't jumped a horse since he had lost his foot, and the prospect of doing so now was a little frightening, for a fall from a horse, especially on a jump, could result in serious injury. But he pressed the mare forward, hoping that he would keep his seat despite the inability to rely on the stirrups. The mare rose at the obstacle, and for a heart-stopping moment as they flew over the hedge, he was convinced he would fall. But the mare landed smoothly and when she came to a stop, Stephen was still on her back.

Neither Gilbert nor his mule was up to the jump and they expended precious time looking for a gap. Stephen chafed with impatience.

When they had gone perhaps half a mile, Stephen swung toward the river. It took a sharp bend to the north here and another sharp bend east, and in the pocket formed by the eastward bend, Stephen paused in midstream to allow the horses to drink while he studied the fields on the other side. No one was about who might give an alarm.

They came out onto the road out of sight of the town. The field before them climbed a steep hill topped with forest. No one was about.

They rode up the hill and entered the forest. It was cooler here, even though the bright sun flickered through the treeless branches, sometimes with such dazzle that it hurt the eyes when Stephen looked back to see if they were followed.

Stephen continued roughly north, or as close to north as he could given the lay of the slope. After about another half mile from the road, he turned west into a valley. Before long they came to a track which was no more than a series of ruts in the grass and the leaf litter. He turned south along the track. He couldn't be sure where it went, but he doubted it led anywhere but to Clun, probably connecting a hamlet to the north with the town.

A while later, they came upon a man with an ox yoke on his shoulder followed by a boy, striding in their direction. The pair looked alarmed at their appearance and got off the track to watch them pass from behind a tree.

"How much farther to town?" Stephen called to the man.

"About a quarter mile, maybe," the man answered, remaining behind his tree.

"Nice weather," Stephen said.

"So it is," the man said. "What happened to him?" Meaning, Gilbert.

"He got into a fight," Stephen said.

"Looks like they got the better of him. What are you doing here?"

"We got lost."

The man grunted in disbelief, but now that the riders had passed and as it seemed certain that they were intent on continuing to Clun, he came back to the lane and watched until they turned a bend.

It proved to be more than a quarter mile, and after a quarter hour, the top of the town's palisade appeared ahead over a slight rise in the ground to the right. The track turned to follow the crest of the rise, apparently skirting the north wall, heading toward the road to Bishop's Castle at the west side of town.

Stephen left the track, descended the slope, and stopped in the ditch. He dismounted and climbed the embankment to the foot of the palisade. The top of the wooden wall was beyond the reach of his outstretched hand. His original plan had been to stand on the horse to get over, but the embankment was too steep for the horse to keep its footing.

"You'll have to give me a boost," Stephen said to Gilbert.

Gilbert looked weary, but did not protest as he climbed off his mule and braced his back against the wall.

"I shall try not to step on your face," Stephen said as he placed a foot on Gilbert's cupped hands.

"I shall be forever grateful," Gilbert said. "Provided you live long enough to make the effort worthwhile."

It was not necessary to use Gilbert's head as a step, though Stephen did require his shoulders. From that height, he was able to grasp the top of the wall. He chinned himself and peeked over. At the foot of the embankment was a street and on the other side of the street were houses. He saw no one on the road, but that didn't mean that no one might see him. This was the most dangerous part. Anyone seeing a stranger coming over the wall was sure to raise the hue and cry. Stephen had chosen the wall to avoid the attention of the town wardens who rarely patrolled the walls during the day, preferring to keep watch from the tops of the gate towers.

Stephen strained to hang there. He could not last much longer. The risk had to be taken. Stephen threw up a leg, slipped over the top of the wall and stood on the peak of the embankment, where a path ran along the top.

He slipped down the slope to the street and strolled along it, trying to act as if he belonged there. He felt naked without the sword, which he had left with the horse, but that too would have drawn attention to him, since ordinarily it was against local law to go about armed in town. He was nominally gentry so the law did not exactly apply to him, but he thought it was better to blend in as much as he could.

According to what Hugh had told Stephen about Clun, it was shaped like a squashed box. The four streets forming the edges ran by the walls and three streets cut through the middle from north to south. The house he sought was on this upper street somewhere ahead, beyond the rising ground before him.

He passed one side street, then another shortly afterward. At last, over the hump of the hill was the house, notable by its sign, a red needle and yellow thread, on the corner of the third street, which was so narrow it was almost an alley.

It was a simple two-storey house with its shop in front, the shutters down to enjoy the good weather and the prospect of business.

There were three people in the shop. A girl of about sixteen or seventeen had a distaff on her arm and was spinning flax. A woman of about thirty was mending a coat, and the man, whose hair was turning gray, was sharpening a needle.

The girl, braided hair concealed by a linen cap, put down the distaff and spindle and came to the window. She had a round face and a small nose with a spray of freckles across it. Some men might have said she was plain, but she had lively eyes and a bright smile that made her attractive. Stephen felt a pang of dismay at the thought that such an innocent looking girl might be mixed up in murder.

She said, "May I help you, sir?"

"Are you Leola?" Stephen asked.

The smile faltered and the eyes grew wary at the fact he knew her name. "Yes."

"My name is Stephen Attebrook. I'd like to ask you a few questions."

A chill descended upon the shop. The girl's lips pressed together and she seemed to have gained several inches in height. The man put down the needle and came to the window.

"What is going on?" the man said.

"He's from the priory, dad," Leola said.

The man squinted at Stephen. "You're that fellow at the bridge this morning, the one who started the fight. The earl would like to get his hands on you."

The man reached down and came up with a cudgel that Stephen imagined he must keep there to clout disagreeable customers who argued over the prices or the quality of the work. The tailor went through the door to the passage that led from the street to the back of the house and came out onto the street.

"Get him, dad!" the girl said. "We can trade him for Oswic!"

Stephen backed up, worried about the cudgel and wishing now that he had brought the sword. "Oswic has fled," he said.

"What do you mean Oswic's fled?" the man asked.

"Just what I said," Stephen said. "He's not at the priory. He ran away this morning."

"Good for him," the man said.

The girl looked stricken.

The woman, who had now joined the girl at the window, said, "You've got to take him, Edgar. The earl will be furious if you let him get away." She leaned out the window and shouted, "Out! Out!"

The girl joined her in the call.

People's heads poked out of their windows along the street, as far as the women's voices could carry, and within moments men and women began spilling out of the houses. Other voices took up the cry so that it reached the gate on the road to Bishop's Castle and a couple of armed town wardens appeared to see what was the matter and came running.

Stephen backed up as a crowd began to gather around him until he reached the embankment, which was quite steep here. Many in the crowd carried cudgels like Edgar's. Sudden fear made his arms feel leaden. The crowd would surely beat him, but, worse, they would turn him over to FitzAllan. Somehow his dagger came into his hand as his heels detected the rising ground behind him, too steep for him to climb quickly with his bad foot.

The two wardens from the gate reached the crowd and pushed their way to the front. "What's going on here?" one of them asked.

Edgar said, "He's the one who caused the trouble at the bridge this morning."

"How do you know? You weren't there," the warden said.

"He said his name was Attebrook, Stephen Attebrook," Leola said.

"Attebrook, that's the one," the warden said. He made no move, however.

"Well," Edgar said, "aren't you going to arrest him? He's only got that little pig sticker."

"Pig sticker or not," the warden said, "I think we'll send to the earl. We've got him cornered here. He isn't going anywhere."

"Go on, Willie!" someone called. "Get him, you gutless wonder! That's what you're paid for!"

"I'll be having words with you later, Coenred," Willie the warden said. "You didn't see what he did to Tommie and Delwyn. Laid them out like logs, the poor fellows, quicker than you can blink. No telling what tricks he can play with that pointy thing. We'll wait. Unless you want to do the honors."

Coenred did not answer, and Willie said, "I thought not." Willie said to the others, "All right, then. Don't everyone stand there with their dicks in their hands —"

"I'll stand with your dick in my hand!" a woman called.

"Thank you, Maud, I may take you up on that later, if your husband has no objection," Willie said. "Someone get off to the castle, right quick now."

A couple of boys detached themselves from the crowd and ran down to the corner and disappeared.

"Well, then," Willie said, leaning on his spear and keeping a respectful distance from Stephen, "we wait."

The people in the crowd did not notice the commotion at the gate and Stephen was hardly aware of it himself and would not have seen it if the slope of the embankment had not put his head a bit higher than everyone else's.

There were shouts and Gilbert appeared on his mule with Stephen's mare in tow. Someone in the crowd said something. Heads swiveled in Gilbert's direction, and mouths dropped open in surprise and amazement at the sight of Gilbert pounding up the street, jolting about on the back of a galloping mule like a grain sack that had come untied. But what amazed them more was not the sight of Gilbert's horsemanship or that his face was swathed in a bandage, but the fact that he was driving straight at them at a full gallop and swinging a sword.

The crowd scattered as Gilbert drew up. Although he could not help looking clownish — a little round man with his head wrapped in linen who could barely keep his place upon his mule — any fool was dangerous with a sword. Gilbert reined to a halt before Stephen. "Best not to tarry," he gasped.

Stephen leaped onto the mare. The mare and the mule sprang back to a gallop as if stung by lightning. Stephen was aware of Willie the warden in his path still clutching his spear. Stephen snatched the spear from his hands as he went by with a "Thanks, Willie!"

"Fat lot of good you are," someone called.

And in a moment they were out of earshot over the crest of the hill and pounding down the other side.

"What now?" Gilbert asked. "We can't exactly leap over the wall."

Stephen pointed to the right. "The east gate."

They reached the end of the street where it reached the town embankment, turned right and headed toward the river, streaking by a woman with a basket of laundry on her head. The woman stumbled out of the way and dropped the laundry into the street.

"Oh, dear," Gilbert said. "Look what we've done."

"Never mind that!" Stephen snapped.

The road was narrow here, hardly wide enough for one cart or two men on horseback, so that others on foot had to scatter to the margins like the poor laundry woman. The road curved slightly so that they could not see ahead to know what was coming until they were upon it. Around the curve was a cart full of barrels and the mule squeezed around it on the embankment side, Gilbert leaning precariously, almost losing his seat and the sword; Stephen on the house side, passing so close that he had to lay his right leg on the horse's back to avoid scraping it against the timbers of a house.

The street dipped and rose, and just beyond they saw the end of it with the gate tower looming on the left.

The horse and mule bent into the left turn, still at a gallop, heedless of what obstacles might lie in the way, Stephen praying that no carts blocked the gate and that the wardens were asleep.

As they made the turn, Stephen saw with relief that nothing stood in the gate and it was open, as he had expected it to be during a normal, peaceful day. But one of the wardens was there with his spear, and he could cause trouble if he wanted to.

Stephen couched the stolen spear and leaned over as they pounded into the gateway, trying to look as menacing as possible, point directed at the warden's head.

The warden ducked out of the way, and they were through the gate to relative safety.

Stephen tossed the spear away, shouting over his shoulder, "I borrowed this from Willie! He can have it back!"

The warden did not reply.

They slowed to a trot, a gait Gilbert liked no more than the gallop. Fifty yards from the gate they came upon the track to the ford, where a woman was hanging laundry over her fence to dry, and turned toward the priory.

"Got yourself in a spot of trouble, did you?" Gilbert asked, struggling for breath as the animals fell to a walk at the ford. Riding, after all, could be hard work and not only for the mount.

"How did you know?"

"I heard the shouting and knew it had to be you, mucking things up. So I went to the source and looked through the fence. It's badly in need of repair, you know. The rest you saw."

Stephen nodded, angry with himself for the failure of his plan.

Gilbert said, "Well, you could at least say thank you."

"Thank you."

"It does not sound like you really mean it."

"I mean it."

"I don't think you do. I really don't. We've got ourselves in trouble now and you can't even be properly thankful. Sir Geoff will be furious when he hears what a mess we've made. Oh, and the prior as well. Let's not forget our host. You didn't manage to find out anything from that girl, did you?"

"She was too busy urging her father to knock me on the head."

"You could use a bit of that. I'd do it myself, but you're too tall."

"I'll ask Harry to do it for you when we get back."

"If we get back." Gilbert shuddered. "We may have to go outlaw after this. I do not relish sleeping in the forest and eating poorly cooked game."

Chapter 17

The monks of the priory were sitting down to supper when a commotion broke out in the cloister. Anselm's voice could be heard raised in protest and suddenly it cut off with a yelp of pain. At the prior's scowl, one of the novices went to the door to see what was the matter but it banged open just as he reached for the latch, nearly knocking him over.

A pair of armed soldiers entered the room, followed by two knights, one of them Percival FitzAllan. A dozen more soldiers paraded in so that the refectory seemed crowded.

Hugh leaped to his feet. "This is an outrage!"

"No, my dear prior," FitzAllan said, "it is nothing so serious."

"What are you doing here?" Hugh demanded coldly. "We have suffered your depredations and insults but this is too much."

"I have come to apprehend some lawbreakers," FitzAllan said.

"You have no jurisdiction on priory land."

"I have whatever jurisdiction I want. What can you do, throw a book at me?"

"There are no lawbreakers here," Hugh replied, though there was a slight shake to his voice. "Oswic has gone."

"So I am informed. I had in mind two others." FitzAllan pointed to Stephen and Gilbert.

"They have not done anything to merit arrest," Hugh said.

"Don't be silly," FitzAllan said. "You know very well what they have done: assault and battery, trespass on the town, inciting a riot. They nearly killed one of my wardens when making their escape. But justice will not be denied."

"You cannot have them," Hugh said.

"Come, prior, this is not a church. I see no altar here. They have no claim to sanctuary and so may be arrested by the lawful authority wherever they are found."

"I will appeal to the crown!" Hugh said shrilly.

"If you must," FitzAllan said, not moved by the thought of royal intervention. He looked thoughtful. "But I will make an agreement with you. If you turn them over to me without complaint, I will give you access to the Clun market."

Hugh looked stricken and tried to compose himself. He stammered, "And your bailiffs, you will call them off?"

"I don't think there is any need to do that," FitzAllan said. "They are well behaved and will be so in the future."

Hugh swallowed. He hesitated a long time as if fighting an internal struggle. He said, "I will have it in writing."

FitzAllan waved a hand. "There will be no mention of any exchange."

"Of course. But we must have your license for access to the market and your promise that our people will not be molested by your bailiffs. And tolls, there will be no tolls."

FitzAllan laughed. "You'll pay the same tolls as anyone who is not a resident of the town."

Hugh hesitated again. "All right."

FitzAllan sank onto one of the benches and appropriated a monk's ale cup. He drank from the cup and said, "Fetch your scribbler and let's get this done. It will be dark soon."

"He means to hang us when he gets his hands on us," Gilbert whispered into Stephen's ear as the scribe set down the agreement between the castle and the priory. "We'll never see the inside of a court or stand trial on any charges."

Stephen nodded. "I don't doubt that, but I hope that he's not in too much of a hurry."

Four of the soldiers had come around to stand behind them. Stephen's first thought had been to fight, but there were too many of them, all armed while he had only a dagger. The second had been to flee, but it was unlikely that Gilbert could get away and if Stephen managed to gain a window, he was certain that the soldiers had horses and would quickly ride him down. So before they had got in place, Stephen palmed his utility knife, which he used for everything from gutting game to smearing butter. He bent over, removed his boot and slipped the knife into it. The handle of the knife fit in the space his missing toes had once occupied and the blade ran along the side of his foot. The presence of the blade would make him limp, but he did that often enough that he hoped no one would notice or care. While he was bent over as tying his boot laces, one of the soldiers plucked the dagger from his belt and knocked him lightly on the back with the handle.

"Fuck you," Stephen said to the soldier.

"Don't antagonize them!" Gilbert hissed.

"They're antagonized already," Stephen said.

"I don't want to be beaten again," Gilbert said.

"I don't blame you. But I don't see how we can avoid that."

By the time the agreement had been drafted, read and approved, and copies sealed by the parties, sundown had arrived and the bell rang for Vespers. The monks, who had kept their eyes on their food and on the floor so as not to betray their feelings, filed out. Only Hugh, the malefactors, and FitzAllan and his men remained. Hugh glanced over his copy of the agreement, rolled it up, and went out as well without a glance of his own at Stephen or Gilbert. Only tightly drawn lips and an unusual paleness gave away the turmoil that lay within.

"Well," Stephen murmured, "good bye then."

"Oh, dear," Gilbert whispered. "Oh, dear, oh, dear."

FitzAllan stood up. He tossed his empty ale cup on the table. "Bring them," he said, and strode out of the refectory.

Soldiers tied their hands and led them out to the cloister. Lay brothers watched the procession from cracked windows above the west range as they went through the passage, and Anselm was briefly visible from behind the shutters of his window.

FitzAllan and the knight who had accompanied him and three of the soldiers were already mounted and riding out of the yard. The soldiers who had Stephen and Gilbert by the arms apparently had walked from the castle, for they set out on foot toward the village. The people who lived in houses across the road gathered at the verge to watch, their faces solemn in the fading sunlight.

The air was crisp and sharp, hinting that there would be a freeze tonight, but the sky was clear except for wisps of high cloud, golden with the last smears of sunlight.

Stephen limped down to the crossroads at the village church where Alcwyn stood in his gate, oddly looking as if he had just eaten a good meal.

The group turned the corner for the descent to the bridge and here again the road was lined with people — it seemed all of lower Clun had turned out to see what was happening.

Once across the bridge, they took a lane that led to the left around the town wall. It terminated at the high, flat-topped mound of earth that was the castle's lowest motte. Stephen, who had not given the castle a good look, saw it sat in a good defensive spot at a bend in the river, which came down from the north and turned sharply east just before reaching the bridge. It was an unusual fortification. It sat on a series of three mottes, conical flat-topped mounds, each taller than the one before it. They passed into the first and lowest motte, which was surrounded by a low wooden wall. It held a bakery, a barn, a pigsty and houses for the lower castle folk. It connected to the next motte by a wooden bridge. Within the second motte, also surrounded by a wooden wall, there were barracks, a kitchen, an enormous woodpile, a granary and stables and other buildings hard against the walls.

Stephen and Gilbert got no farther than this second motte. Stephen had a glimpse of the third and highest, capped by a whitewashed stone wall enclosing a square stone tower. It was an old tower and had a crack clearly visible running up the side. Behind the old keep was the shell of another under construction.

The soldiers removed the binds and pushed him and Gilbert into a low timber structure and locked them in.

It was pitch dark inside and the ceiling was so low that Stephen bumped his head. He stumbled from the blow and stepped on something that moved beneath his foot.

"Watch it!" a voice said in the darkness.

"Sorry," Stephen said.

"Welcome to my castle," the voice said. "It used to be a pigsty before the pigs acquired new quarters, but I call it home."

"It smells like pig," Gilbert said.

"You'll get used to it," the voice said. "Mind the ceiling."

"I've already met its acquaintance," Stephen said, sitting with his back against a wall.

"Good for you," the voice said. "What have you done to insult our lord, if you don't mind my asking?"

Gilbert said, "My friend here beat two of FitzAllan's men at the bridge this morning and we are accused of starting a riot in the afternoon."

"I heard about that. I don't get much news here, but when I press my ear against the door, sometimes I hear things. That caused quite a stir."

"What I can't understand," Gilbert said, dismay in his voice, "is why the prior betrayed us."

"The prior betrayed you?" the voice said with clear interest.

"We were guests of the priory. He could have protected us, but he gave us up to FitzAllan in exchange for rights to the Clun market. How could he do that?"

"The better question," Stephen said, "is why FitzAllan would make the offer. He hates the priory. Denial of access to the market is central to his plan to strangle it. Why would he give that up?"

"This is interesting," the voice said. "Our lord certainly hates the priory. No doubt about that."

"I don't know," Gilbert said.

"When I was at Llwyn's yesterday," Stephen said, "I saw kegs of salt with the same mark we found on those stolen by the robbers on the Shrewsbury road."

"You didn't tell me about that! You don't think —" Gilbert said, letting the full thought hang in the air.

"That FitzAllan is behind the robberies on the Shrewsbury road," Stephen said.

"Why would you think that?" Gilbert asked.

"FitzAllan needs money," the voice said. "That tower of his has cost more than expected — the first one fell down and he's been forced to try again. He's raised rents on all his tenants to the point they are near to starving, and he does not suffer a debt to go unpaid. In my case, he has imagined a debt that does not exist, and holds me until it is paid. I would not put simple robbery beyond him."

"Exactly," Stephen said. "His neighbors will not be pleased to learn he has been preying on commerce through their lands. So he wants to silence us."

"But what reason could FitzAllan have to know that you suspect him?" Gilbert asked.

"Llwyn had dispatched the kegs to Wales for sale," Stephen said. "I saw the pack train leaving with them. I questioned the guards where the kegs had come from, and they said FitzAllan. Later I saw one of the guards in the yard. Apparently he had come back from the train and spoke to Llwyn about my interest."

"And Llwyn told FitzAllan?" Gilbert said.

"Most likely. If there is an inquiry into the robbery and suspicion focuses on them, they both fall," Stephen said. "Protecting himself from a capital charge may be more important to FitzAllan than his dispute with the priory. Besides, he can renege on his promises at any time."

"He wouldn't do that," the voice said sarcastically.

"Of course not," Stephen said. "Lords never go back on their word."

"Well, then, you shall surely hang," the voice said. "Just be so kind as not to give out that you've shared your secret with me. I only owe him money, and as soon as my wife gets it, I'm a free man."

"I have no intention of hanging," Stephen said.

"Glad to hear that," the voice said, "but I don't see how you can avoid it. Our lord always gets what he wants in the end."

The night was cold within the former pigsty, and Stephen did not get much sleep. When dawn arrived and light seeped through the cracks in the timbers, he could see his breath. He peered out one of the cracks. The bailey was busy with people moving about, grooms saddling horses, a blacksmith banging on a piece of iron, the kitchen staff hustling to complete dinner with bustle everywhere and smoke pouring from the chimney.

He turned from the crack to see that the voice in the dark had a face: a man nearing middle age with more than a week's growth of beard and straw in his brown hair. The man sat up, rubbed his face and removed the straw from his hair, which he combed with his fingers. He grinned at Stephen. He said, "I always like to look my best for the gaolers."

"You have a blanket," Gilbert said with envy.

"Here that makes him a rich man," Stephen said.

"I am rich enough on the outside as well," the man said. "Unfortunately that is what attracted our lord's attention."

"How so?" Gilbert said.

"He wanted a loan. When I would not give him as much as he wanted, he seized me until I produce it, and calls it a debt. Slippery things, words. It's funny how they can mean whatever you want them to. Night is day, day is night, a loan is a debt, taxes are gifts, a fair share is whatever the lord wants it to be. At least I will not hang." The man grinned. "He knows enough not to eat the sheep that produces his wool."

"You're a wool merchant," Stephen said, hazarding a guess.

"My, you are sharp this morning. Reginald Blasingame is my name. And yours?"

When they had introduced themselves, Blasingame said, "So you're an Attebrook. I'm surprised. That's a good family.

He must really be worried about you. At first, I thought that he might actually want to hold you for ransom. Now, I'm not so sure. You are in a real pickle."

They spent several hours in conversation, for there was nothing in the gaol to do but talk or use the pisspot. Toward midday, a servant collected the pisspot and left them with a fresh one and a pitcher of water, and shortly afterward, the door opened to admit a woman. She was well dressed with a thick green cloak, and had a strong but pretty face. The white streak of a widow's peak showed below the rim of her wimple. She had a basket under her arm and she knelt and put it on the ground by Blasingame.

She said, "You have guests, Reggie."

"They decided to drop in last night," Blasingame said. "Gentlemen, this is my wife, Anna."

"You are the people who caused the disturbance in town yesterday," Mistress Blasingame said when Stephen and Gilbert had been introduced.

"Regrettably so," Stephen said.

"And you are strangers with no friends or family here," she said. "A pity." It was a pity because they would have no one to bring them anything to eat as she had done for her husband. Gaolers did not ordinarily feed their charges. She began laying out the contents of the basket on Blasingame's lap, for there was no clean space on the ground and she did not spare a napkin: bread, cheese, several hard boiled eggs, an apple, and a sausage.

"Enough talking in there!" a voice called through the open door. "Hurry up."

"I'm coming," Mistress Blasingame called back. She said to her husband, "I saw a curious thing this morning on my way into town."

"Oh?" Blasingame said.

"All the stock was gone from Llwyn's lower pasture, every cow, every horse and every sheep. He's never done that before, that I can remember. I wonder what he's done with them. Sold them, do you think?"

Stephen's hair seemed to stand on end. "You have a house west of town?"

"Yes," Blasingame said. "We just bought one there, a little manor of our own. Why?"

"Then you best take everything you own and make for the forest," Stephen said.

"Why should we do that?" Mistress Blasingame asked.

"The Welsh are coming."

"A warning like that must be worth something," Gilbert said, eyeing the collection of food after Mistress Blasingame had departed.

"It would be if it were real and not a false alarm," Blasingame said. "Uprooting our business and carrying everything off to the wilderness costs a lot of money." He saw the grim expression on Stephen's face. "What do you know?"

"I have spoken with Llwyn," Stephen said. "I know what he intends if there is trouble in the March."

Blasingame brooded. "Well, I suppose you are entitled to a share, but I have nothing to divide it."

Stephen removed his boot and produced the knife, which he passed to Blasingame, who cut up the sausage, cheese, apple and bread. Blasingame returned the knife and tossed each of them an egg besides.

Stephen cleaned the knife and returned it to its hiding place.

They ate in silence for a while. Blasingame said, "Will this be a mere raid or will it be an army?"

"An army," Stephen said.

Blasingame nodded. "There has been talk of that. The weather's been mild. An army could take the March by surprise this time of year."

"That must be Llywelyn's intent," Stephen said.

"The Welsh burned Clun once before," Blasingame said. "When I was a boy — thirty years ago, now. The town gave them no trouble, but the castle held out, although it was sorely damaged. It's stronger now, too, with the high motte walled in stone. It will be even harder than before."

Stephen recalled a conversation he had overheard about ladders. It had made no sense at the time, but now its import seemed clear. Knowing exactly how high to build scaling ladders was one of the challenges of siegecraft. Disaster and death were the fate of attackers whose ladders were too short.

He did not share his thoughts with the others, but brooded on them for some time. Loyalty to the crown demanded that he warn FitzAllan of the possibility of attack and how it might be carried out. But going before the earl in a way that implied he meant to bargain for his life struck hard against his pride. When all a man has is pride, it can twist his thoughts out of shape. So Stephen sat on the gaol floor and stewed, pulled one way and another, hating FitzAllan and hating himself.

Chapter 18

The remainder of Saturday passed without incident, relieved only by the humming of the flies which managed to get through the cracks in the timber walls and by intermittent conversation among the imprisoned.

As the day wore on Stephen withdrew from conversation and fretted about ways to get out of the gaol. He conceived of one plan after another, but none seemed workable, and some were outright fantasy. In truth, his mind was a mire of anxiety and out of such muck came little that was useful. He had to calm down. Otherwise, no plan would come.

By sundown it grew cold again. Blasingame wrapped himself in his blanket. Stephen and Gilbert, who had no blanket, huddled together more for the imagined benefits than from any actual warmth they were able to share.

Sunday came with nothing to relieve the monotony of confinement. A servant boy rather than the mistress brought Blasingame's dinner, and the guard allowed in neither him nor his basket, and confiscated the cargo, so they got nothing to eat — or any news about what Blasingame's family was up to. But the fact the wife had sent a servant in her place was enough to give Blasingame comfort that his goods and family were being looked after.

Night fell again and a quarter moon made silver slits of the cracks between the timbers. Stephen did not huddle immediately with Gilbert but looked out through a crack at the deserted yard, letting his thoughts wander. They were more settled now, less driven by fear. More focused.

Eventually, he lay down beside Gilbert and tried to sleep. Sometime toward dawn, he woke up and groped to the pisspot. As he relieved himself, he heard a faint sound, like the knock of one piece of wood against another: so faint that he thought he imagined it. But something about the sound alarmed him. He crept across the gaol to the far wall, mindful not to step on Blasingame. He looked through a crack in the gaol wall. It was too dark to see anything except the outline of the embankment and the palisade against the starry sky.

A figure appeared at the top of the palisade. The figure jumped down onto the wall walk. It was rapidly followed by another and another, until a stream of figures could be seen all along this part of the wall, and voices could be heard talking in harsh whispers.

"What is it?" Gilbert asked, sitting up.

"The Welsh have come," Stephen said. "They've got in the fort."

"Now?" Gilbert asked, startled.

"A night attack," Stephen said with admiration at the enemy's boldness. "A surprise."

"What do we do?" Blasingame asked, fear and disbelief in his voice.

"Nothing. Hope we are not noticed."

"Dear God," Blasingame said.

Voices were raised in shouts and the thud of swords against shields and the ting of swords against swords could be heard as battle erupted within the fort.

The fight in the middle motte did not last long. The Welsh were over the wall in such overwhelming numbers that the small garrison did not stand a chance. Four soldiers who managed to survive the initial assault and arm themselves retreated to the bridge to the upper motte, but the Welsh had attacked that as well with scaling ladders, and such a mass of the enemy had swarmed between the upper and middle mottes that the retreat of the survivors was cut off and they were massacred upon the bridge.

Stephen and the others watched the Welsh go from building to building, looting and killing everyone they could find. A party of Welsh came to the gaol but, owing to its resemblance to a pigsty and the foul odor, went away, to the relief of the prisoners who hoped that by the time anyone thought to investigate again passions would have cooled enough that they might survive.

Anxious, sleepless hours passed until dawn.

The Welsh took over the middle motte as if it had belonged to them all along. Someone started the fires in the kitchen and began cooking, while others cut wood for that fire and similar blazes that were kindled in the hall.

Some enemy soldiers brought out the bodies of the dead and piled them in a heap in the yard. It made an impressive and ghastly pile: men, women and children all thrown together.

Meanwhile, there was a great deal of activity at the gate to the lower motte, much coming and going that suggested to Stephen that the enemy had taken that fort as well. No doubt the town had fallen also. But from the prisoners' limited vantage point, they had no way to know for sure.

A large party came through the lower gate pushing a tree trunk that had been fitted with cart wheels. They pushed it to the gate to the upper motte and waited there for a considerable time. Bugles blew and there were shouts outside the walls, joined by those within as a crowd of the enemy gathered around and behind the tree. Heaving and shoving, they pushed it through the gate. Apparently, the night attack had been thrown back and the enemy was trying again.

There was more shouting from the direction of the upper motte as this attack went on, punctuated by the muffled pounding of the tree on the gate. But within half an hour the tumult died down and those who had gone through the upper gate came streaming back, carrying dead and wounded. They lay the dead out in a row and carried the wounded into the hall. This attack had failed too.

There were no further attacks, and the enemy settled into a siege. The middle motte filled up with enemy troops and there must have been many more outside — thousands, even:

a huge army for a country where most armies numbered no more than two-hundred men.

Tents were erected in the yard around a bonfire on which the enemy stacked wood and gathered about in large numbers after supper for drinking late into the night. The drinking started before sundown, since the garrison in the high motte was so small that no one seemed to think a sally possible.

Stephen watched for a while, then sat with his back to a wall, thoughts of escape occupying his mind again. If they could get out, the chances of mingling unnoticed in this mob were far better than when the English had held the fort. Some of the timbers were rotten, perhaps enough that he could chip a hole with his knife wide enough to fit through. He crept across the gaol to the far wall, which faced the embankment and took out his knife. He began prying splinters loose, careful not to make too much noise in case there might be a lookout on the walk above them.

Gilbert, meanwhile, watched the proceedings in the yard. Presently, he said, "Stephen, come look."

"At drunken men? I've seen enough of them before."

"Not these drunken men. Hurry, before you miss them."

Reluctantly, Stephen abandoned his work and crossed to kneel beside Gilbert.

"There," Gilbert said, pointing. "That's Oswic, or I'll be damned."

Stephen nodded grimly. "It's him all right. And those fellows with him, the two peas from the same pod, they look familiar — they are Alcwyn's boys."

"The priest? The priest of lower Clun?"

"I know of only one Alcwyn."

Gilbert crept to the wall and peered out with Blasingame, who said, "Ah, those three. Thick as thieves they've always been, and always getting into trouble."

"Good heavens. They've gone over to the enemy," Gilbert said.

"They are the enemy," Stephen said. He told Gilbert about the conversation concerning ladders he had overheard on the way back from Llwyn's.

"Why didn't you mention it before?"

"I didn't think it was important."

"Dear man," Gilbert clucked. "It was most important indeed."

"I see that now," Stephen said, annoyed at the reproof.

Stephen crawled back to the far wall, but only got half way, when Gilbert said, "Someone's coming."

"Here?" Stephen asked.

"I do believe so."

Stephen could hear several voices outside. Someone rattled the lock. Then someone kicked the door, but it was a stout door and held easily. Figures were visible through the cracks crouching down to get a look inside the gaol.

The men outside spoke in Welsh to much laughter and someone said in Welsh-accented English, "How's it going in there, boys? Are you comfortable?"

"Could you please let us out?" Gilbert called back. "We've been in here for days without food or water." That wasn't strictly true, of course. But a day in this hole could feel like several.

"Water," the man who had spoken now said in Welsh, "the fool wants water! Let's give him some."

There was a spattering sound and Gilbert jerked back from his crack.

"They pissed on me!" he said with disgust and dismay

Outside there were gales of laughter. Even Blasingame seemed to find it funny.

"I'll thank you not to laugh at me," Gilbert snapped at him.

"Sorry," Blasingame said, covering his mouth so no one could see any smile that might remain.

"They don't mean to let us out," Gilbert said, as the Welsh went away.

"So it would appear," Stephen said. "Nor feed us either." He resumed chipping at the timber. "You could use some slimming down anyway. I won't have to make this hole so big."

"I am slim enough, thank you very much." Gilbert clasped his hands on his ample stomach and sighed. "What I wouldn't give for a bowl of Edith's mutton stew. I don't expect I shall ever see her again. It is a pity."

Chapter 19

"Do you think she will remarry," Gilbert mused, "after I am gone?"

Three days had passed since the attack, and Stephen had managed to make a hole in the timber. But the log had proved to be more hardy than he had expected and the hole was big enough only to get his arm through it. He said, "You say that as if you minded."

"No, of course I don't mind," Gilbert said in a tone that suggested that he minded very much. "It's just . . ." His voice trailed off.

"You're jealous," Stephen said, continuing to hack away at his hole. By the time it was big enough for any of them to fit through, they would all likely be dead of thirst.

"I am not," Gilbert said.

"She was married before, wasn't she?"

"What if she was?"

"Well, then, she probably will again."

"It makes me feel . . . disposable."

"I suppose we are, husbands and wives alike." Some men certainly treated their wives as if they were disposable, going from one to another as each of them died or, in the case of men who did not bother with marriage, cast them aside when they wearied of them. Stephen thought of his Spanish woman, Taresa. There was nothing disposable about her: she had been irreplaceable. Her death had left a chasm in his heart that nothing could fill, not another woman, not drink, not time. Women and drink brought only moments of forgetfulness. He felt as though he would never be whole again. There were times when he resented Gilbert's happiness with Edith — no, it wasn't resentment. It was envy.

"Hurry up with that hole, damn it!"

"I'm tired. It would help if you'd take a turn for a change."

Gilbert crawled across the gaol. "Out of my way."

Gilbert chipped away throughout the afternoon. He made no more progress than Stephen had done, however. But he kept at it with focus and determination, his breath coming in puffy jets as the temperature dropped to freezing.

From time to time, Stephen watched the goings on in the yard, as gray clouds rolled in, coating the sky with a solid slate cover like the lid on a pot.

He noticed that tiny speckles of white were drifting out of the sky. Just as it dawned on him what was happening, Gilbert turned from the hole and said, "It's snowing."

"You better work faster," Stephen said. "We don't have much time now."

"What do you mean?"

"It means that the Welsh will be leaving soon," he said. "And if we're still here when they're gone, FitzAllan gets hold of us again."

"That will not happen!"

It snowed gently throughout the night, and by morning when they awoke, a thin blanket of white covered everything, even the tops of the fences. And the snow still came down, harder now, in sheets that intermittently obscured the far wall of the motte no more than sixty feet away.

The camp in the yard came alive with activity. Officers shouted at the men, who struck the tents and loaded them and all the loot that had not already been carried away on pack horses that had been brought up from the town. Before long the tents were down, the pack horses and men began to file out, and nothing remained in the yard but the remains of the bonfire, which still burned, and a snowy mound that was the dead castle folk.

As the last of the men and horses were leaving, a large group of the enemy came back with buckets from the lower motte. The group split up and the men began pouring and swabbing the contents of the buckets on the buildings and the palisade walls. Stephen's breath came short in his throat when he realized what that stuff was — pitch. The Welsh were going to burn down everything in this motte and beyond.

Already through the snowy haze a billow that was neither cloud nor snow could be seen rising from the direction of the town.

"They've fired the town," Stephen said.

"They have?" Blasingame said in anguish. "My poor townhouse. I really liked that house."

"You can build another," Stephen said.

"We won't get out," Blasingame wailed. "They mean to burn us alive."

A party of Welsh reached the gaol as he spoke, and a pair of them slung bucket-loads of pitch on the roof. Driblets of the tarry black stuff seeped through cracks in the planks and plopped on the rotting straw that served as their floor. Gilbert and Blasingame regarded the driblets with horror.

"This will keep you warm!" one of the Welsh said through a crack, and then they were gone to the next building.

"Let me at it!" Blasingame said and seized the knife from Gilbert and attacked the hole, which had not got much larger from last night. He hacked at the wood, sinking the knife deeply into the log, and, when he attempted to pry loose a large chunk, it snapped in two. Blasingame stared at the stump of the blade with horror.

"Look what you've done!" Gilbert howled.

"Keep going," Stephen said. "What's left will have to serve."

Blasingame glanced at him guiltily and continued his attack with what remained of the knife.

A shadow tugged at the corner of Stephen's eye and he looked through his crack. A man stared back at him from the other side.

"Father Alcwyn," Stephen said. "For some reason, I am not surprised to see you here. What do you want?"

"I've come to offer you confession," Alcwyn said.

"Can't you let us out for that?"

"I'm afraid not."

"Confession," Stephen mused. "How thoughtful of you."

"I have always tried to be a good priest. I've not always been successful, but I have tried."

"I think I would rather talk about your sins than mine," Stephen said. "Let's talk about William."

Alcwyn was quiet for a moment. "What do you want to know about Brother William?"

"Did you kill him for the money? You had to know about it."

Alcwyn scratched his beard. "Oh, I knew, of course. Caerwen talked enough about it and how he was going to build a life for them when he left the priory."

"Did you object?"

"No. He was a good boy, really, smart, with lots of talent. He would have done well wherever he landed and taken good care of her." He sighed. "It was not about the money. My dear daughter, she does not know when to keep her mouth shut. She sings like a bird. Whatever thought comes into her head she has to speak about it."

"She told him what you and your boys were up to," Stephen said. "Making the ladders for the attack."

Alcwyn nodded. "That night we had visitors from the west. They came to my house by the church. It seemed a better place to put them up than at the farm, given the sort of men they were. The farm would have been an insult. Caerwen went to the church that night to see William as she did most nights. She told him about the ladders. She said to me later that she only wanted him to get the money so they could leave right away, before the trouble started. But he came to my house to confront me, and the visitors were there, hard proud men from Powys, they were. They told me to have him killed before he gave the alarm and spoiled the plan. It all depended on surprise, you see. We would find out how tall the ladders needed to be and they would take the castle by surprise during the night. Surprise was everything."

"And you went along."

Alcwyn shrugged. “I did not have a choice.”

“What did they promise you?”

Alcwyn hesitated. “A priory of my own in Wales.”

“But the Welsh did not kill him.”

“No, that was the boys, Brin and Bran. They wanted the money if William had to die, but William was surprisingly stubborn. He would not tell, no matter how hard they beat him. It was as if he could win somehow if he did not tell. Eventually, the Welsh got tired of hearing him cry out, and feared he would wake the neighbors. So Brin cut his throat.”

“Whose idea was it to put William back in the priory?”

“I am afraid that was mine. Caerwen had told me about the hole in the wall, and it was an easy thing to throw the body on a horse and take him back there. We knew that Oswic would say nothing. He and my boys have been friends since they were babies.”

“A clever way to throw off suspicion.”

“I thought so. It only had to do so for a short time.”

“And it was Brin and Bran on the road to Llwyn’s?” Stephen asked.

“Yes, they are impulsive. Are you ready to confess?”

“Not to you.”

“What of the others?”

Stephen glanced at Blasingame and Gilbert who had listened to the conversation with wide eyes. They shook their heads.

“We’ll take our chances with Saint Peter,” Stephen said.

“So be it,” Alcwyn said. “I am sorry, you know. I hope you will forgive me.”

He rose and strode rapidly through the falling snow to the lower gate.

Chapter 20

All that remained of the enemy was a party of about twenty armed men who guarded the gate to the upper motte. A cart appeared from the lower motte followed by another twenty men or so. The cart bore torches and the Welsh dipped them in the last of the bonfire. They fanned out across the enclosure.

Some of the Welsh entered the buildings while others set fire to the roofs, which were made of thatch. The careful way they held up their torches to the thatch reminded Stephen of a servant lighting candles in a hall during the evening. Thatch is nothing but bundled straw or sticks and is usually dry and vulnerable to fire, and this thatch was no exception. Everywhere the Welsh applied flame, the thatch kindled and began to burn. At first the flames were small, little fingers of incandescence hardly visible in the haze of snow, and Stephen prayed that the falling snow and the wind would snuff them out. But it was a vain hope, for the flames quickly grew in size and fury, spreading across each roof with malevolence, curling, fuming, bright with destruction.

Those who had gone inside did not tarry, and not long after they came out, flames could be seen licking within the windows, reaching toward the ceiling, no doubt feeding on pitch that had been smeared over the dry wood of the structures. Even the gate house to the upper motte was not spared, and within a short time, fires glowed through the windows on the ground and first floors and even crawling up the interior sides where pitch had been spread like butter on bread. The rear guard withdrew from the gate as the flames there grew in size and fury, until they were burning so strongly that no could pass through or put them out.

Other men turned their attention to the walls, spreading fire all around the enclosure so that the fort acquired a ring of smoke and flame.

As the fires grew in intensity, the Welsh began departing until there were only a few of them left. No one had yet bothered with the smaller sheds or the gaol, but now it was their turn, as if someone had remembered what had been overlooked in their hurry.

One of the Welsh threw a torch at the gaol. It turned end-over-end as it wheeled toward them, the fire on the pitch-soaked moss tied to the end whooshing and nearly going out. The torch struck the edge of the roof and fell to the ground. But the thrower came forward and tossed it upon the roof and ran for the gate to the lower motte, his work done.

The prisoners stared at the ceiling of the gaol, panic in their hearts. They could see yellow flame through the seams between the roofing boards where the caulking had fallen out. It was only a matter of time before the roof caught full afire and roasted them.

Stephen stood as much as he was able and put his hands against the planks overhead. They were already warm.

Gilbert and Blasingame turned toward the hole and hacked at it with a fury propelled by fear. But the wood was as hard as ever. They would not be able to get through in time, no matter no matter how much they tried.

Stephen sank to his knees, trying to compose his mind for the end. There did not seem to be any point in being afraid of the inevitable. He told himself that he just had to accept it and hope that it was not too painful. He knew death could be gentle, even violent death. When he had lost his toes, he had felt the blow rather as a knock on the foot. There had been no blaze of agony, no incapacitating sparkle of pain. In fact, he had been able to fight on and engage two men before it had sunk in that he had been crippled, even killed, for men were not expected to survive such wounds, and he would not have lived if it had not been for Taresa. And his experience was not unusual, for he had known men who had been lucid and calm with arms and legs cut off, until they finally died.

He looked out one of the cracks into the yard. All the buildings in view on fire.

Across the way, he saw a rat appear and dash away from one of the buildings. Then another, and still more, a flood of rats fleeing the fire. They seemed to spring from the ground itself.

And it hit Stephen — they were coming out holes in the ground under the walls.

"Dear God," he said to himself, "I am the greatest fool."

He scrabbled along the ground at the edge of the wall. The ground was hard packed. His fingernails made only bare scratches in the earth — not easy digging with bare hands.

"Bring that knife!" Stephen shouted to Gilbert and Blasingame. "Hurry!"

"What?" Gilbert shouted back.

"A hole!" Stephen said. "We must dig a hole!"

Gilbert hesitated, and lunged across the gaol. He understood right away, and began jabbing at the hard ground with the stub of the knife to loosen it as Stephen scooped handfuls behind him like a dog.

They worked together side by side, Blasingame hovering anxiously behind. The hole grew slowly in size despite their combined efforts, but it grew, inches at a time, a bit deeper, a bit deeper, a bit deeper.

A hole appeared in the roof and cinders of fiery pitch dripped through and ignited the straw on the floor.

Blasingame dived on the burning spot and smothered it with his blanket. But more cinders fell through as the hole widened and smoke seeped through the cracks in the wood. They could feel the heat from the roof as if they were in an oven. It would not be long before the roof collapsed on them. Blasingame used the blanket to push the rushes to one end of the gaol, leaving only bare floor for the cinders to fall upon.

"Hurry, for God's sake!" he cried.

Stephen and Gilbert had gone down a foot by now, but the planks of the wall had been planted in a trench that went down at least that far. But at last they reached the end of the sunken wall and dug beneath it.

The heat grew so intolerable that they began to sweat from it and the smoke became choking so that they could barely breathe even with their mouths buried in their collars.

The tunnel now curved under the planks of the sunken wall. There was room in it for only one of them now. Stephen took the stub of the knife and hacked at the earth with one hand and scoped out what he had loosened with the other. It was cooler in the earth and easier to breath, and he dug furiously.

At last the tunnel turned upward. Loosened earth fell into Stephen's face so that now he seemed to smother from it rather than the smoke, but death by earth seemed cooler and therefore cleaner.

Finally a plot of ground gave way upon him and as he cleared it, gray sky, filled with flame and smoke, appeared above. Stephen ducked back into the gaol. He shook Gilbert, who lay with his lips pressed to the earth, on the shoulder. "Come on!" he shouted, the roaring of the fire almost smothering the words.

At first Gilbert didn't move. But then he looked up with rheumy eyes and nodded.

Stephen wormed through the hole.

He turned to help Gilbert, but instead saw Blasingame's head at the bottom of the little pit. The man's body jerked back and forth and he made no effort to pull himself through, and Stephen realized the man was unconscious and Gilbert was attempting to push him through, a thread that did not want to go through the needle.

Stephen grabbed Blasingame's shoulders, dragged him out, and laid him on the snow, the man's mouth gaping toward the sky as if in death, but his chest rose and fell, the only indication that he still lived.

Gilbert appeared now, but he only got as far as his shoulders. "I'm stuck," he said.

Stephen grasped Gilbert's arms and pulled. But Gilbert did not budge. After much fruitless tugging, Stephen squatted over the hole, reached in, and adding the strength of his legs.

"Suck that stomach in, damn you!" Stephen cried.

"I'm sucking!" Gilbert wheezed. "I'm sucking! Good God, you're tearing me apart! Leave off! Let me go! Save yourself!"

Stephen gathered his strength one more time and heaved for all he was worth. Gilbert gave way an inch, and a few more with a second heave, and with the third he came out with a pop so that they fell together, almost landing on Blasingame.

Stephen lay there for a moment.

Then he looked around.

The buildings were consumed by flame everywhere in the fort. Sheets and tongues and great fingers of fire covered the sides of all the buildings, and the roofs had become enormous caps of writhing flame reaching at least a hundred feet in the air, so high it seemed as though they might melt the clouds — the entire middle motte was one vast pyre all around them, the falling snow melting to a fine mist, mingled with ash and cinders.

"Now what?" Gilbert panted.

Now what indeed? For even the gaol was a mass of flame and the heat from all around was so intense that Stephen felt as though it might cook him like a pig on a spit. The heat had melted all the snow in the yard, leaving puddles of mush everywhere, but none of them was deep enough to provide a refuge.

There seemed to be only one place to hide and the prospect was hideous. He pointed at the pile of corpses and said, "There."

Without waiting for a response, he got up and stumbled across the yard to the pile, passing a swarm of rats which were huddling together in the very middle of the yard, seeking to use each other as a shield from the fire.

He knelt by the pile and hesitated. The snow had melted from the pile, leaving only patches here and there, and the naked bodies of the dead were a ghastly gray and blue. Many had died with their eyes open, which now looked upon with world with a ghoulish glaze. Many had terrible wounds on their faces.

"Forgive me," Stephen said, and burrowed into the pile.

He felt the others burrowing in beside him. He closed his eyes, and for the first time in more than a year, said a prayer.

There was nothing to do now but wait.

The fires burned throughout the day. Now and then they felt the earth shake and heard thunderous crashes as one building after another collapsed. But they did not dare look out to see the spectacle. Only after nightfall did Stephen risk exposing his head for a look. All around fires still burned, low now, but intensely hot, glowing eerily in the night, illuminating the whitewashed walls of the upper motte with a reddish hue.

A gray, overcast dawn greeted them when they at last felt safe to push out of the pile. The proud buildings which had stood as symbols of the earl's strength were now only piles of smoldering rubble. The buildings had made a solid rank around the wall and embankment and even now there was no way through them. However, the gaol was less of a wreck than the others, and Stephen led the way up to the embankment through its remains, holding his breath from the smoke that rose from the embers. The palisade had burned as well, but only in spots, so there were gaps like the teeth in a beggar's mouth. Stephen paused at a gap and looked at the upper motte. A pair of heads were visible upon the wall. He and the sentinels regarded each other for a moment, and he slipped through the gap and clambered down the steep side of the motte.

They had come down on the river side, and worked their way along it among the burned out wreckage of more buildings. They reached the street leading to the bridge, and Blasingame said, "I think I will leave you fellows here."

He gazed up at the remains of the town wall, which has as full of gaps as the castle's palisade, some burned, some pulled down. "My poor town," Blasingame said.

He climbed up the embankment and disappeared into the ruins of the town.

"A pity," Gilbert murmured.

The Welsh had left the bridge intact and its planks were covered in mud from the passage of the retreating army. Their path in flight was obvious, for the road along the river leading west was a ribbon of mud so thick and churned up that it was hard to imagine how a man, a cart or a horse had managed to pass along it in the end. Indeed, down where the road curved a cart had been abandoned in the muck.

Nothing but black heaps remained of the houses of lower Clun. The taverns by the bridge, and the houses along either side of the street leading up the hill, were smoking hulks just like those in the castle.

Stephen and Gilbert walked slowly up the street. At the first bend where the village petered out, they reached the church. It was still standing unmolested, as was Alcwyn's house, although the door gaped open. Driven by hunger, Stephen searched the pantry, the buttery and the kitchen, but everything had been removed. The only things alive in the house now were echoes.

They continued down the road to the priory, hoping that it too had been spared.

But it had not. The half-built church still stood, looking more a ruin than it had before, but the priory close was burned down, leaving soot stains on the stone of the church, as had the buildings across the way. Even the windmill was gone.

So far, they had seen not one living person but the castle watchmen and there was no one here either.

Stephen and Gilbert sat on the stone wall marking the boundaries of the priory to absorb the magnitude of the calamity and to consider what to do. They could not remain there long, though, for it was cold and they had no protection.

"I suppose we should make for that last village we passed on our way here," Stephen said. "Clunton, I think its name was. It can't have been more than three miles away. They should have food if the Welsh haven't taken the trouble to raid it."

Gilbert hopped from the fence. "Let's get started," he said, without enthusiasm at the prospect of a long, cold walk.

Stephen joined him in the street and they turned toward the ford.

A robed figure emerged from a copse at the junction with the lane that led south to where the windmill had stood. The fellow waved and ran toward them. They saw it was Brother John. His pock-marked fact broke into a happy smile — much too good humored for the circumstances. "You survived," he said when he reached them, "by the Grace of God."

"I suppose it was," Stephen said.

"Of course. I prayed for you," Brother John said. "Wait here. You must be famished. I shall fetch something to eat."

Chapter 21

Brother John returned with a pair of cloaks, a loaf of bread and the prior.

Behind Prior Hugh came a stream of people, some from the priory, some from the village.

"Brother John said that the enemy has gone," Hugh said to Stephen, whose mouth was full of bread.

Stephen continued to chew and did not answer.

"How did you live?" Hugh asked.

"They left us to burn," Stephen said coldly. "But we dug our way out after they left. And you?"

"We led the village people to shelter in the forest," Hugh said, waving a hand behind him.

As they stood there, more village folk came through on the way to see the remains of their houses. Stephen exchanged glances with the tavern girl, Aelflaed, who nodded in greeting but did not speak as she went by.

"We will move the camp here," Hugh called to the folk.

"Do you have any more to eat?" Gilbert asked, still chewing furiously on his half of the loaf.

Hugh nodded. "We managed to save most of our stocks and our animals."

"How?" Stephen asked, surprised.

"Llwyn sent a warning," Hugh said in a low voice so that no one else could hear.

"You were lucky," Stephen said.

"We were," Hugh said. "But I've lost the priory. I don't know how we shall rebuild. We don't have much money. And now we have barely enough to get everyone through the winter. I am sorry. I truly am. I regretted what I did from the moment I spoke. I was tempted and I was weak. FitzAllan offered what my heart desired most and I could not refuse. I of all people should have been able to do so. I do not deserve to be prior or to lead these people. Will you forgive me?"

Stephen fingered the last of his bread. "Someday, maybe."

Hugh looked at the ground. "I deserve your contempt. I know that." He waved at a monk who emerged from the lane leading Stephen's horses and the mule. "Here," Hugh said to Stephen. "I saved these. I return them to you now."

Stephen greeted the horses and noted that all his gear was tied to the pack saddle where it should be.

He said, "Do you have a shovel?"

Amazingly, one of the workmen found a shovel among the ruins. Stephen shouldered it and his sword, and entered what had been the priory yard. He located the gate into the cloister, and took a couple of paces north. He crossed the blackened, smoking timbers that had formed the wall. Everything but the supports had burned pretty thoroughly so there wasn't much bulky debris. He estimated his spot and probed the ground with his sword. Presently, he handed the sword to Hugh, who had followed him into the mess, hopping from one foot to another because the ashes beneath them were hot.

"What are you doing?" Hugh asked through the hem of cloak he held over his mouth so that he could breathe.

Stephen did not reply.

He began to dig.

It did not take long to uncover the box.

Stephen carried it out of the ruins and lay it on the ground in the yard. It was very heavy and a strain to carry it even that far.

He knelt and opened the box.

Inside was a hoard of silver pennies.

Stephen looked up at Hugh and said, "Brother William's treasure."

"How did you know it was there?" Hugh said, astonished.

"He hid it in the safest possible place — under his bed."

"It's a fortune," Hugh breathed.

"A small one," Stephen agreed, "but a fortune nonetheless." He added, "He died for it."

"What?" Hugh asked, dumbfounded.

"Alcwyn's boys, Brin and Bran, tortured him to reveal its location. He died taking the secret with him."

"It wasn't FitzAllan after all?"

Stephen shook his head. He closed the lid and stood up, the box under an arm.

Hugh stared at the box, and across the valley of the Clun to the ruins of the town, where smoke still rose in many places. He said, "I give it to you. In compensation for my sin against you."

Stephen considered what Hugh had said. The box held what had to be four or five pounds in money, an enormous sum that he could live well on for some time. The prospect of decent clothes, of regular hot baths, of pliant whores, of a room that was not in an attic in which he risked bumping his head just by standing up — all that was intoxicating. The possibility of that and more lay upon his tiring arm.

He put the box upon the stone fence. He said, "Build yourself a new priory and see that these folk don't starve."

Hugh's mouth fell open and he put his hand upon the lid. "You're serious?"

Stephen nodded. He mounted the mare and turned her toward the river. "Good day to you!" he said without looking back.

Gilbert caught up just before Stephen reached the ford.

"I'm proud of you," Gilbert said.

Stephen glanced at him with a slight smile. "Oh, shut up. And don't you ever say a word about this to anyone. Especially Harry."

Together, they splashed through the ford and turned onto the road to Ludlow.

Chapter 22

Knowing of the rift among the English barons and smelling weakness, Llywelyn ap Gruffydd, Prince of Wales, attacked castles all along the March at the end of November in an effort to drive the English out of Welsh land. The same night as the attack on Clun, both Cefnllys castle near Llandrindod Wells and Knighton fell to surprise assaults by escalade. Presteigne and Norton also were taken as well as many lesser places.

An English army led by Earl Roger Mortimer marched out from Wigmore to recapture Cefnllys, not that there was much to take back. Cefnllys had been built of wood and the victorious Welsh had stripped it of everything of value and burned it. They had begun to march off when Mortimer appeared, and in a sharp battle under the motte of the castle, Llywelyn broke the English, who sought refuge within its ruins. The Welsh took Cefnllys under siege, as they did at Clun and other castles that they had not been able to seize in the first assaults.

Mortimer's army had few provisions left after the defeat, for they had abandoned their baggage in the rout. The men ate their horses and looked out upon the besieging Welsh with dismay and trepidation.

Then the snows came and with them a reprieve. Llywelyn offered to let Mortimer and his ragged survivors return to Wigmore on the promise of the surrender of Cefnllys and all the lands around it. Lacking tents or food and observing the growing host around the motte that suggested an assault to come, Mortimer had no choice but to agree.

Elsewhere along the March where the Welsh were not victorious, one siege after another was lifted as the enemy crept back to their mountains and forests, unwilling or unable to stay in the field in the face of bitter weather. The evacuation of Clun was only one tragedy among many where the Welsh came, looted and burned, only to withdraw, leaving behind ravaged lands and little food for those who had lived there.

It was not the end to the war, only a lull until spring and better weather.

The outbreak of war made the borderlands even more unsafe and dangerous. Few dared to cross from one country to another, and many who tried disappeared and were not heard of again.

Still, Stephen had intended to attempt a crossing. But after delivering Gilbert safely home, Walter Henle, the constable of Ludlow castle and deputy sheriff, had required him to remain as part of the garrison of the castle and town, due to the widespread fear that the Welsh might strike Ludlow. So, Stephen had stayed and worried, and when he was not standing guard or training the town militia, drank more than he should have. He was morose and ill tempered and everyone at the Broken Shield stayed out of his way. Even Harry, for whom business was surprisingly brisk owing to the many refugees from the countryside and who in consequence was in a better mood than anyone, did not try to raise Stephen's spirits.

In the second week of December, a visitor appeared at the Shield. After he had shaken off the snow from his shoulders, he asked for Stephen. Edith Wistwode pointed him out across the hall. The visitor sank onto a bench beside Stephen and warmed his hands over the fire.

"That feels good," the visitor said.

Stephen shrugged.

"You're Attebrook?" the visitor asked.

"What if I am?"

The visitor held out a folded piece of parchment.

Stephen fixed his eyes on the man, who was English by his speech. "What's this?"

"Llwyn asked me to deliver it."

"His warning to Sir Geoff is a bit late."

"It isn't for Randall. Or about the war. It's from someone you know."

Stephen put down his cup and accepted the letter. He broke the seal. He read the words slowly, as his eyes had trouble focusing. It was from his cousin in Wales with the news that they were far from the fighting and Christopher was safe.

Stephen let the letter fall to his lap. "I can't afford to pay you," he said.

"That's taken care of," the visitor said. "My lord sends his regrets at your misfortune."

Before Stephen could reply, the visitor rose and left the inn.

"What was that about?" Edith asked.

"Nothing," Stephen said. "It's about time for supper, isn't it?"

"Soon," Edith said.

"It's a long way from Broad Gate in this weather," Stephen said, more to himself than to Edith, as he rose and stuffed the letter into his belt.

"I suppose it is," Edith said.

Stephen draped his cloak over his shoulders and went out to the yard. He crossed to the stables, where he put a halter and saddle pad on the youngest mare.

He led the mare into Bell Lane. At Broad Street, he turned down the great hill toward Broad Gate. Harry was visible just inside the gate, wrapped in a blanket.

"What do you want?" Harry asked when Stephen stopped before him.

"It's supper time," Stephen said.

"So?"

"Gilbert and I have a bet." Stephen lied. "I say you can ride better than him. He expects you to fall off. I've come to see who's right."

Harry eyed the mare with reluctance. "You expect me to ride that?"

"Exactly."

Before Harry could say anything, Stephen gathered him around the waist and lifted him up. Harry was solid muscle and much heavier than he looked and it was a strain, not helped by Harry's squirming and the pin-wheeling of his arms. But Stephen managed to get him on the mare's back.

"You're drunk," Harry protested. "I will not be the butt of a drunken prank."

"You don't have a choice," Stephen said.

Harry clung to the mare's mane. "It's a long way down," he said anxiously.

"If you fall, just be sure to land on your head," Stephen said.

Gip, the gate warden, stared at the spectacle from the safety of his nook.

"What are you looking at?" Harry glared.

"Nothing," Gip said. "Nothing at all."

Harry gauged the distance back to Bell Lane with a calculating eye. He made that trip at least twice a day and knew every pebble on the way. It was not a hardship for someone able to walk, but it was a long, hard trip on his board. He assumed a lordly air and waved jauntily at the driver of a cart descending the hill to the gate.

Stephen tugged the mare's halter rope, and, with Harry's board on his shoulder, he started back up Broad Street, feeling much better than he had in a whole month.

87295215R00113

Made in the USA
Columbia, SC
11 January 2018